John Dunbar Hylton

Betrayed

A northern Tale

John Dunbar Hylton

Betrayed
A northern Tale

ISBN/EAN: 9783337174569

Printed in Europe, USA, Canada, Australia, Japan

Cover: Foto ©Andreas Hilbeck / pixelio.de

More available books at **www.hansebooks.com**

BETRAYED:

A NORTHERN TALE.

IN SEVEN PARTS.

———

BY

J. D. HYLTON,

Author of "The Heir of Lyolynn, &c., &c.

PALMYRA, NEW JERSEY,
1880.

DEDICATION.

A son have I, a ruddy boy,
All full of health and life and joy,
Whose burly form doth promise give,
If he to man's estate should live,
That we a healthy man shall find
Alike in body and in mind.
He drives his goat, his pony rides,
Like perfect horseman, him bestrides;
Flies forth on him o'er hill and dale,
Leaps broadest ditch and highest rail;
Leaps with his dog, or him outruns,
Nor any danger shirks nor shuns;
Swims on the stream, or rows his boat,
And shouts the songs he has by rote.
Does everything I bid him do,
To me is always kind and true;
And while on winter nights my time
I spent in building up this rhyme,
Beside my chair his own he drew,
His blue eyes fix'd on me their view,
And as I wrote each couplet down,
I saw him either smile or frown—
Just as it chanced his list'ning ear
Did plain or not my mutterings hear;
For as with verse I paper don
Aloud my song I always con;
It seems to give it smoother flow,
And make my song more rapid grow;
And when a couplet pleased his ear
He would repeat it loud and clear.
This rhyme alone amongst this host
Has always seemed to please him most:
" Forward the stream of time has drawn.
To gulfs that never cease to yawn."
Both night and day I hear his voice
Repeat aloud and oft his choice.
With me he'd sit right late at night,
Till drowsiness o'ercame him quite;
Then on the lounge he'd sink to rest,
His burly arms across his breast;
And when Aurora's rosy car
Lit up the east and paled each star,

DEDICATION.

From off the lounge he lightly sprung,
Around my neck his arms he flung,
Upon my lips his kisses press'd
And me all tenderly caressed;
Then bade me read him every thought
That I through night in ink had wrought.
While this I did, I saw his eyes
Sparkle with joy or deep surprise—
Display in it an interest strong,
Which might to fuller years belong—
Yes, yes, to one of man's estate;
So to him this tale I dedicate.
He is my best and truest friend,
And his I'll be till life shall end.
Yes, through all life or death for him
I'd shun no peril, dark nor grim,
No mortal nor immortal woe,
And he the same for me will show
Through every varied change of fate.
Let my success be small or great.
So this, and all verses I create,
I do to him them dedicate
May love of God by him be won,
And every blessing crown my son.

———*———

PREFACE.

About a year has ta'en its flight
Across this realm of day and night,
Since I brought forth through joy and
    pain,
Another vintage of my brain
I styled the BRIDE OF GETTYSBURG.
Whose metre charmed John Odenswurg,
A friend of mine, whose hand and pen
Is foremost 'mongst the sons of men ;
Whose mind soars o'er the noblest walks
Wherever knowledge sings or talks ;
Whose judgment ever stands supreme
'Mongst men, whatever be the theme ;
Who is a critic sharp and keen
As ever in this sphere was seen,
But void of all things base and mean ;
Whose spirit knows no spite nor spleen,
But is of every baseness clean
As is the purest gold, I ween,
That ever gleamed on hand of queen,
Or rosy lass of seventeen.
I've never known his soul to lean
To'rds that grim monster all obscene
Whose eyes they say are bleared and
    green,
With flaming tongue foul lips between.
Whose haggared features plainly show
I's servile nature, grim and low,
Where never thought nor deed did glow
To comfort joy or solace woe,
Which ne'er heroic feeling felt
And where no thought of courage dwelt ;
But is all low, depraved and vile,
Concentred mass of fraud and wile.
Yes, void of jealousy is he,
As is the carn that breaks the sea ;
And brave is he as is the rock
That backward turns the billow's shock.
And this friend of mine, John Odenswurg,
Pronounced my BRIDE OF GETTYSBURG
A noble tale, from end to end.
As ever yet by man was penn'd ;
Sublime in thought, in action grand,
Let the scene be on flood or land—

All, all, was limned to nature true,
Whate'er the figure, shade or hue—
The grass within my story grew
The way that laughing nature knew.
And flowers bloomed upon the earth,
As they in nature found their birth,
The mountains reared their peaks on high,
And o'er them spread the sacred sky
Just as they are in nature seen,
With winter's rime or summer's green,
The floods gushed forth in streams or rills
As they gush over nature's hills;
The ocean looked, in calm or storm,
As in the lap of nature warm.
And when the human heart I drew,
I painted it to nature true;
Limn'd it in either ill or good
As it has aye in nature stood.
My battle scenes were limn'd complete,
In either triumph or defeat;
As swept the tide of verse along,
The cannon thundered in my song,
And plain the charger's neigh was heard,
As death and tumult round him stirr'd;
And defeat, victory, or death,
Rolled from the drum or trumpet's breath.
Thus speaks my friend, John Odenswurg.
About my BRIDE OF GETTYSBURG.
And yet I do not thank him more
Than other critics, full a score,
Who said my tale was full of fault,
Did all in rhyme and nonsense walt,
From end to end all lame and halt—
Tasted like bread all void of salt
Mixed with sand or flinty gault,
Or porter with no taste of malt.
That mouldering lies in the vault,
That will in silence waste away
When vats that hold it shall decay.
I do not care if good or ill
The critics speak of me. I still
In heart and soul shall feel the same,
Let them bestow me praise or blame.
I know my tale is really good,
And if 'tis rightly understood
By those who read it through and through.
They'll view my verse as it I view
And credit me as is my due—
Bear witness what I say is true;

They'll see it is not full of fault,
Nor in the least way lame and halt,
But sturdy, native strength is thrown
In every line unto them shown,
And none of feebleness is known
In any of its flow or tone.
Those who praise, give but what's my due
And tell me what I know is true ;
And while I thank them for all this,
Yet I feel, nor do I feel amiss,
Nor am I it ashamed to tell,
That I have really paid them well
For all the trouble, praise and time
They've spent a'conning o'er my rhyme ;
For surely, they have in it found
Some things that made their spirits bound
With sorrow, joy, delight or hope,
Or made them altogether cope.
Perhaps they far better spent their time
A'reading o'er my flowing rhyme,
Than had it never met their view,
Nor vital breath its author drew.
To those who blindly me condemn,
I'd speak a word, or two with them :
If me they'd only deign to meet
Within some classical retreat,
I'd still their jealousy awhile,
Make reason through their beings smile.
If e'er with them I chance to meet,
A gallant friend or foe they'll greet.
And with my mind and spirit fraught
With just such feelings and such thought,
I send forth on the stream of time
Another tale in flowing rhyme,
Which I, its father, style BETRAYED,
Nor feel I for its success afraid.
Go forth, my child, upon your course,
You o'er the world your way shall force ;
Nor shall human hands your progress mar,
Nor you from your just glory bar.
Press on ; I'll put you to the test ;
I've blest you, and you shall be blest.
Pres on, press on ; your sire's arm
Shall shield you from all dole and harm.
The good will hail you with a zest,
And bless you, as you I have blest.
You shall not beg, but force your way,
And nothing fear by night nor day

BETRAYED.

PART I.

I.

Autumn's lazy mists spread soft and still,
With amber hues o'er sky and hill ;
The setting sun all bright and fair,
With yellow glory fills the air;
Gives unto hill and dale below,
An all-bewitching, crimson glow.
And sweet does sparkling rill and stream
Reflect the fast departing beam,
O'er trees where frost but late has been,
And turned to red their leaves of green;
Huge gums and oaks and maples tall,
Poplars vast, scrub-wood dense but small,
The sun bestowes his parting glow,
Makes all the hues of fire show ;
Like sparks of flame amidst the glare,
Their leaves at times fall on the air—
Far from their parent stems repair,
Then spark-like, make on earth their lair
Along the base of those bright hills,
Whence gush a hundred rippling rills,
Which form a river broad and clear
Of waters pure as ever were;

Whose shallow crystal ripples show,
The pebbles white o'er which they flow.
And pastures broad and rich and green,
On which are herds of cattle seen,
And bleating sheep by thousands graze,
O'er fields that midst the sun-set blaze.

II.

High on the mountain's rocky side,
O'erlooking all the pastures wide,
There stood, built of dark-gray stone,
A mansion fair as e'er was known.
Its stately walls and slated roof,
To flame and rain and storms are proof.
Full many a spacious room, I ween,
Is in that stately mansion seen.
It looks all like some castle-hold
Reared by some gallant prince of old,
Save that no battlements are there,
Such as round ancient castles were;
But all around are porches seen,
And o'er them crawls the ivy green;
Near by are walks with hedges trim,
And stately trees of giant limb,
And gardens that in summer time
Breathe round a fragrance all sublime.

III.

Upon its porch the owner stands,
And gazes o'er his fertile lands;
Happy is he, no care he knows,
For not a cent to man he owes;
O'er all his home and pastures broad,
He is the sole and only lord;

No dime to any man owes he,
Though in his debt full many be.
Large is his heart and kind his soul,
And charity his thoughts control;
Good will he bears the human race,
Whate'er their station, call or place.
No mortal ever sore in need
Of aid, to him did vainly plead;
If gold they craved he gave the hoard,
Oft more than he could well afford;
To them many a loan he made,
Which unto him was ne'er repaid;
O'er such losses he'd ne'er grieve nor fret,
But give the borrower the debt.
To losses he was aye resigned,
And soon would cast them from his mind;
Far o'er the country was he known,
As one who ne'er called in a loan.
Though hard to gain his wealth he'd toil,
And made it all from out his soil.
His beaming face and smiling brow,
Tell plain that he is happy now;
That not a care disturbs his soul,
And placidly his feelings roll.
His clean-shaved, ruddy cheeks disclose
The perfect health that through him flows;
From their hue strangers might divine
Their florid color came from wine;
But none of this e'er made his fare—
'Twas perfect health that reddened there.
His stalwart form and brawny limb
Shows you no man more strong than him;
His form and limbs all, all reveal,
A perfect man from head to heel;

Though from his look it plain appears
That he is well advanced in years;
For his thin hair is white as snow,
Or foam that rolling billows show;
But if not for their milk-white rime
He'd look like one in hardy prime,
So stalwart is his look and tread;
But five and sixty years have fled
Since dawned on earth that rosy morn
When was this man, John Logan, born.

IV.

The broad domains his eyes survey,
And many herds that o'er them stray,
Were now the grand reward and spoil
Of his own thrifty, constant toil:
Yea, all the lands and home he'd won,
Came through the patient work he'd done;
All had been gained by his own hands—
His mansion, herds, and fertile lands,
And God he thanked, his actions showed,
For what to him He had bestowed.
Beside him now his daughter stands,
And on his shoulder rests her hands,
Looks on his ruddy face the while,
With happy heart and loving smile;
Bare is her head of scarf or hood,
Her tresses bound with silken snood,
Her long thick curls of light brown hair,
Sport freely on the balmy air.
Her form is slender, frail and tall,
But graceful, and majestic all.
Fair is her forehead, broad and high,
And 'neath it darts a hazel eye;
Her ruby lips reveal to sight

Her even teeth all pearly white ;
Her rosy face, her ruddy cheek,
Do her own perfect health bespeak ;
All o'er her face from chin to brow,
Such beauty ne'er was seen till now
Since first the lovely race began,
And came to bless and comfort man.
The hues of blood and driven snow,
In mingled shades divinely glow ;
Each strives the mastership to win,
O'er all that face from brow to chin.
Her swan-like neck and bare round arms
Compete with all her glowing charms,
And like the milk-white mists are fair,
That near the moon's full disk repair,
And o'er her seem to make their lair,
Or float at night in moon-lit air ;
And light her tread, as fleecy snow
The cloud-land sends to earth below,
Her voice is soft, and sweet and low
As music in its sweetest flow.
And ne'er a soul more good and pure
Did ever human flesh immure.]
A tear she had for other's woes,
And sorrow o'er her soul arose,
While pity all her being stirred
Whene'er a tale of grief she heard.
She was that country's boast and pride,
And famed for beauty far and wide ;
Yea, prized o'er all that country's range,
Was Mary of the Logan Grange.

V.

And happy might John Logan be,
With such a daughter as was she ;

In owning such a glorious child,
One so gentle, pure, and meek and mild ;
A paradise his home she made,
And all his cares to rest she laid ;
Made all his days serenely pass,
As sunshine o'er his fields of grass ;
Or in one even tenor glide
As crystal rill down mountain si...e,
On which no ruffling tempests blow,
Nor falls no chilling winds nor snow ;
But by it rose and lily glow,
And form in arches o'er its flow,
While summer suns eternal shine,
And cheer it down its steep incline.
If faults in either one were seen,
As are in humankind, I ween,
They never troubled either mind,
For both to such seemed always blind.

VI.

Within his child he sees portrayed,
With every grace and charm arrayed,
The image of that lovely one,
Long years ago he woo'd and won ;
That lovely maiden pure and mild,
He'd made the mother of his child—
The lustre of whose hazel eyes
Was pure and bright as dew that lies
On the flower at early morn,
When first the sun doth it adorn—
Pure and serene as is the light
The stars shed on a frosty night,
Which only tell of peace and love
Within their silent vaults above.

And straight his memory is cast
Adown the vista of the past,
Far swifter than the sunbeams pass
Along a field of waving grass,
Cast through the cloud's dark, broken
    form,
That speeds before the mountain storm ;
And all his joys and woes of yore
Pass through his musing soul once more
As through the past his musings range,
It rises up with all its ceaseless change,
And limns a panorama strange.
And midst its scenes his daughter, there,
Who smiles so blooming, grand and fair,
With all her mother's peerless charms,
He sees a babe brought to his arms—
Like on that bright and happy day,
When first he did his child survey.
Yea, hailed his first-born with a joy,
Nor time nor care could e'er destroy:
Hailed her a gift sent from above,
To crown his days with peace and love.
The joyous thrill his bosom knew
When first to him the tidings flew
That he a father was, once more
He feels as holy as of yore.
A year of time flies on, again
He hears the nurse's voice amain
Shout unto him with teeming joy—
His second offspring is a boy.
Feels as of old through all his form,
The blood sweep pulsing swift and warm ;
In thought he climbs the winding stair,
Doth to its mother's couch repair,

And on the twain he plants once more,
The loving kiss he gave of yore;
His soul feels with that joy assailed,
As when his second born he hailed,
And o'er his features beams the while,
Just as of old, his tender smile.
Two years sweep by, that boy he sees
A little prattler on his knees,
With azure eyes just like his own,
An image of himself is shown,
In all that infant's features pure,
Which years shall strengthen, not obscure.
O'er dale and hill he leads his child,
Till comes a night with tempest wild ;
Though falls no rain fierce roars the storm,
And flying clouds the sky deform.
Sudden a glaring flame is seen,
Below amidst his pastures green,
And swift a roaring fire glows
From out a barn that there arose ;
Right soon is wrapped its stately frame
In one all-devouring flame.
From out his couch with speed he hies,
And to the scene of ruin flies ;
While round the burning wreck he toils,
The flames of other buildings foils ;
Tears down the gates and fences all,
Around those burning structures tall,
And from the flame's terrific ray
Swift drives his frighted herds away,
To stables hastes, and from each stall,
Leads out his trembling coursers all,
And saves all things his hand can find,
That some one had to flame consigned.
While thus he toiled, the very hands
That there had cast the flaming brands,

An entrance to his mansion found,
His wife they seized, and gagged and
    bound,
And while she thus all helpless lay,
The boy the ruffians bore away.
The night sped on, and morning came,
Still Logan fought the roaring flame ;
The barn was all to ashes burned,
Ere he unto his home returned,
And all the horrid tidings learned
Of what had in his absence passed.

VII.

O'er all that country wild and vast,
Like dust that flies before the blast,
The fearful news spread far and wide,
And men flew forth on every side.
To find that child, none, none delayed,
In search were neighbors swift arrayed,
And everywhere keen search was made ;
By day and night, o'er hill and glen,
Through woods and swamps and robber's
    den,
Through city, hamlet, town and shed,
The feet of searching thousands sped.
And though they searched that country
    round,
No trace they of the infant found ;
E'en through ships on the sea they sought,
But not a single trace they caught ;
Although they offered huge reward,
To those whoe'er the child restored ;
And swore that those who did the deed,
Should of their fearful crime be freed,
And should to them be paid the meed,

If they returned the child with speed.
Though this was widely noised abroad,
Yet, yet the child was not restored.
The days and months flew on apace,
Yet of the child was found no trace;
A year sped by, another flew,
Yet of the child was found no clue.
The mother wept and prayed and yearned,
Yet, to her arms no child returned.
Its solace Hope at last denied,
And with her grief the mother died.

VIII.

This is a scene in Logan's life,
Which, with sad episodes is rife.
But though the cruel, dreary past
Has many sorrows round him cast,
He has survived them, and looks back
Along his life's long, gloomy track,
With lesser, far, of grief than joy,
Which time doth strengthen, not destroy.
Heavenly hope assails his soul,
Keeps all his thoughts in sweet control.
Looks on his sorrows of the past
As trials God has round him cast
For some all-wise, divine intent,
Which only for his weal were meant;
Which God will yet to him make plain,
And for each loss give ample gain;
And lead him to that blissful shore,
Where he shall meet his lost of yore,
Whom here on earth he did adore;
And they shall meet to part no more;
Yea, meet each cherished one again,
Where dwell no parting, grief nor pain.

Swayed only by these hopes, he lives,
And unto God his thoughts he gives—
Breathes on at peace with God and man,
Aids all his fellow-men he can.

IX.

The sun goes down, and Logan's eye,
Enraptured views the crimson sky,
For rifted clouds around him lie,
And these receive his reddening dye;
Seldom a pageantry more fair,
The setting sun made nature wear;
Bright o'er the heaven's vast expanse
His yellow glories upward glance—
To every far off cloud advance,
Till all the arch divinely glows
With the mellowing hues he throws.
On mists that o'er the mountains spread,
And veil from sight each summit's head,
His brightest tints effulgent glow,
And hues of gold and amber show.
So bright and long the splendor lasts,
The setting sun on nature casts,
It seems his flight he stays a while,
To shed o'er all one loving smile—
Make earth and sky together blaze,
Beneath the splendor of his rays.
Make all things in nature wide,
Their many hues of darkness hide;
And all in sweetest tints be shown,
Although a splendor not their own;
Force Nature through her boundless clime,
To confess his power sublime.

X.

From Logan's sight the sun has sped,
And all that pageantry has fled,
Not e'en one tint the heavens show,
Of all that dazzling pomp and glow;
But over sky and earth below,
The darkening shades of evening grow;
Fast o'er each mountain's shaggy head,
The moving mists begin to spread—
Dark, dense and vast to vales repair,
And settle o'er their nightly lair.
While from the pastures broad and green,
The herds are homeward moving seen,
And sheep with lambs that skip and play,
Come bleating on their homeward way;
And throng the ample folds below.
Those hills' green sides and bases show
Where enormous barns and stables rise,
As ever met a Granger's eyes.
Come from the pools the noisy geese
To pens and settle down in peace;
To stately roosts the poultry fly
And crowd upon their perches high.
The air grows moist with breath of kine,
And noisy with the squeal of swine.
While waiting for their corn and hay,
Is frequent heard the horses neigh.
The corn within the manger falls,
Hay placed in racks along the stalls,
The grunting swine receive their fill
Of moistened bran and floods of swill.
Amongst the gentle, lowing herd,
The sprightly milkmaids' feet have stirr'd,

Ceased are the lively songs they trilled,
While with recking milk their pails they
　　filled ;
And to the milk-house down the hill,
Into which flows a rippling rill,
As clear as crystal, cold as snow,
That milk is placed in cans that glow
Like pure and polished silver sheen,
And as is polished silver, clean.
And all the toil and work is done,
Which comes on after set of sun ;
And over dell and mountain's brow
The shades of night are settled now,
And scarcely can John Logan trace
Midst growing gloom his daughter's face,
As thus she breathes within his ear
What none but him she wished to hear.

XI.

" Father," she said, " I would not give
Earl Ragan for all men that live ;
And if I ever wedded be,
He'll be my lord, and only he.
His soul is noble, good and kind,
As ever God to flesh consigned ;
His eyes are full of truth and love,
And azure as the skies above ;
And though he poor and humble be,
Yet, he is dearly loved by me ;
And with none other will I wed,
Far sooner would I join the dead."
" Your love for him I will not chide,"
The Father with a smile replied,
" For truth to tell, in him I see,
A noble spirit, frank and free ;

Though poor he is, he is the peer
Of all the youths who journey here,
And seek to woo my daughter fair.
Poor, did I say? no, no, my child;
As poor, he can no more be styled.
'Twas I who loaned him all the hoard
With which he bought his acres broad.
One-half of it he has restored;
And every mite he won through toil,
And from the yielding of that soil.
If he repays me at the rate,
He has been paying me of late,
In two years he'll own his whole estate;
And not a man save me, he owes,
Is solemn truth, your father knows.
And just suppose I now should whim,
To cancel all I hold 'gainst him;
He'd the wealthiest wooer be
'Mongst all who come my child to see.
And ere shall rise to-morrow's morn,
That mortgage shall to shreds be torn;
I will forgive him all the debt,
Though of it I'll not tell him yet.
In truth I really like the lad,
And that you love him I am glad.
But there is that gay Crawford Storm,
Of handsome face and agile form,
With garb forever neat and trim,
How will you free yourself from him?
For it is whispered far and wide,
My Mary is his promised bride.
And if one word of this be true,
If he's at all beloved by you,
First see that love is sere and dead,
As leaf the stem past ages shed,

That wasted on the rock is seen,
And never can again be green."

XII.

Bright flashed the maiden's eyes with pride
Night could not from her father hide,
And on her cheek the color died,
As with a frown she thus replied :
" Though such reports are whispered wide,
By me they have been oft denied ;
For they are false, as void of truth,
As is a rock of love or ruth.
Oft have I wished he'd keep from here,
And o'er our threshhold never dare ;
Respect to him I simply show,
Because I would not have him know
The deep contempt for him I feel,
Lest he some harm to us might deal.
I hail him as some loathsome weed,
Of which our garden must be freed ;
When time a proper chance shall give,
He'll learn it, truly as we live.
But think not, father, I will wed,
Ere many years shall yet be sped—
Till Ragan every mite has made,
He owes to you, and it has paid ;
When this has my own Ragan done,
And not till then, his bride he's won.
A solemn compact we have made,
And it shall stand though long delayed—
When he his lands from debt shall free,
Wed on that very day are we.
And he by his own thrift and toil,
No other means must win his spoil ;

Far, far too proud of soul is he,
To take your gift, though grand it be;
Though years of toil 'twould him relieve,
The gift I know he'd not receive;
So ne'er such thoughts to Ragan tell—
You'll shortly see him prosper well;
For day and night to God I pray,
That He will Ragan bless alway;
And far more things through prayer are
        wrought
Than of this world has ever thought.

XIII.

Now, just two weeks have ta'en their flight
Since Crawford Storm last met my sight,
And when he left he said to me,
This evening here again he'd be;
And I have vowed not to be thrown,
Within his company alone.
This very eve, by my request,
Here will gather many a guest;
Yea, all the neighbors far and near,
Both old and young will gather here;
You seem to have forgotten, quite,
That you are sixty-five to-night—
Or, of the day that you were born,
The anniversary came this morn;
And while to-day away you were,
I have prepared more ample cheer,
And summoned all the neighbors here.
When lights are lit you'll find each board
With choicest food is amply stored;
And should sly Crawford come to-night,
You'll see how him I'll shun and slight;
And all the neighbors, young and old,

Shall my contempt for him behold.
And all such tales are false, they'll see,
That I am Crawford's bride to be.
They'll see that Ragan has my love—
Is prized all others far above,
And only, me as bride shall win."
At this her father swift broke in:
" My daughter, do not so to-night,
Nor show to him the least of slight;
That you do naught, I would prefer,
To forth the neighbors' gossip stir;
Oh, bring not this upon your head,
Their gossip is a thing I dread;
For, be you pure and white as snow,
Ere from the cloud it falls below—
That in the ether has its birth,
Nor yet has ta'en one taint of earth,
'Twill not let you pass, whate'er you do,
Without your share of scandal, too.
Leave Crawford unto me alone,
Nor be to him your feelings known;
Of him you shall be shortly rid,
His presence here I will forbid.
And then, I trust, he'd keep away,
Nor ever near you dare to stray.
This eve I shall engross him, quite,
Give you no cause to show him slight."

XIV.

While thus they spake, adown the hill,
Were voices heard, and laughter shrill,
And tramp of steeds mixed with the sound
Of jolting wheels o'er rocky ground.
The sounds came nearer, and more near,

Till Ragan's voice could Mary hear.
"Father, they come," the maiden cried,
And like a flash, flew from his side—
Sped from the porch into a room
That all was filled with growing gloom,
There, swift a lamp she lit, whose light,
Through casements burst upon the night,
And down the mountain's rugged side
Poured forth its lustre far and wide ;
Placed it just where its welcome ray,
Would guide her guests upon their way—
Just where it showed the rocky road,
Which up the slope reached her abode.
From the porch also, Logan sped,
Upon the path his daughter led ;
And as he left, from out a nook,
O'er which dense leaves of ivy shook
Unto the passing winds of night,
But kept all in concealed from sight,
A man of tall and stately frame,
All noiseless as a spectre came.
There for long hours he had been,
By neither child nor parent seen,
Although so close he was his hand
And arm all space had 'tween them spann'd.
And every breathed and whispered word
That they had uttered, he'd o'erheard.
From out the spot he'd lain concealed,
He moved, and night his shape revealed.
Tall was his form, but spare and lean,
Though it had toil and fasting seen,
'Twas all so bony, tall and gaunt,
It seemed a wreck of care and want.
Yet, yet as there he moved along,
His motions showed that he was strong ;

His form erect from heel to head,
And firm and rapid was his tread.
Forth from the mansion swift he strode,
And gained an unfrequented road ;
There paused and on the casement gazed,
From where the light so sheenly blazed.
That light upon his features glowed,
And all his visage plainly showed,
As from his head his hat he drew,
And on the casement fixed his view ;
His clean-shaved cheeks were thin and pale,
White as the snows of winter's gale,
And wore a fixed and rigid air
Of wretchedness or grim despair ;
Yet comeliness his features bore,
In spite of all the gloom they wore ;
His upper lip was robed with hair,
Black as the cloud of midnight air ;
But when he smiled it plainly showed,
The pearly teeth that neath it glowed.
And o er his haughty, comely head,
His wavy locks were thickly spread,
And sable as the darkest shade
E'er nature from her colors made.
And back from his high forehead tossed,
That looked as cold and white as frost
Cast near sable rocks along the hill,
Which makes it seem far paler still.
Dark were his brows, and underneath,
Like sabres flashing from their sheath,
His sable eyes shot forth their light
As flaming meteors of night,
That send afar their piercing ray,
Filling beholders with dismay.

Long stood he gazing on the light,
That through the window streamed on
    night,
And saw that gay and merry crowd
Of neighbors with their laughter loud,
Come up the road, a goodly train,
And in the mansion pour amain ;
Heard plain the sounds of merriment,
That joyous in that mansion blent ;
Heard Mary's voice, so sweet and soft,
Midst tones of pleasure mingling oft.
And listening there he stood the while—
Showed neither sign of frown nor smile,
Until he did Earl Ragan view,
Who last within that mansion drew ;
Then beamed his eyes with fiendish light,
And turned his face a paler white,
His features donned a horrid leer,
As might some cruel spirit wear.
A tremor pass'd through all his form,
And shook it like a reed in storm ;
A muttered curse on air he threw,
And from the scene in haste withdrew ;
Burning with envy, hate and wrath,
Swift down an unfrequented path,
Which lead unto a clump of wood
That far below that mansion stood,
Where he that eve his steed had tied,
He did through gloom securely stride ;
But ere he half-way trod the course,
Which lead to where he'd tied his horse,
Upon the air such thoughts he cast,
As foremost through his spirit pass'd.

XV.

" Yes, yes," he muttered, wild and hoarse,
" My craft and wile shall yet find force
To quench that pure and spotless flame,
She did this eve for Ragan name ;
Yea, she shall loathe and hate him more,
Than such for me she ever bore ;
And she shall from his presence tread
As from some hissing adder dread ;
She shall despise him, soul and form,
Or my name is not Crawford Storm !
And I will make her love me more
Than yet for Ragan e'er she bore.
And her old sire yet shall know,
On me he dare not insult throw ;
Nor me from out his mansion spurn,
Howe'er may Fortune with me turn ;
And ere a day goes by, I trow,
He will respect me more than now ;
And ere one fleeting month shall go,
No slur on me he'll dare to throw.
Yes, yes, my schemes and plans are laid,
Against Earl Ragan all arrayed ;
I'll bring on him a storm of shame,
And Mary yet shall loathe his name ;
I'll bring him to the gallows grim,
Or prison cell shall welcome him ;
And there for his whole life shall stay,
Nor ever more shall cross my way.
Since Mary's love for him I see,
And not a thought she'll give to me,
Now, all too little is this sphere,
For him and I to dwell in here.

Since by open means I cannot thrall
With love the one I love o'er all,
By wile and craft and fraud, I will,
Though basely I a man may kill;
And ere to-morrow's sun shall glow,
A dungeon grim shall Ragan know.
I thought him captured long ere this,
And something must have gone amiss. ·
But I must speed me forth and see
Why he this night from cell is free."
While thus he speaks, his steed he gained.
The strap untied, his courser reined,
Then on him swift his form he cast,
Unto his flanks the rowels pass'd,
And through the gloom he galloped fast.
As cloud that flies upon the blast.

XVII.

Two miles and more had Crawford rode,
From where the lights at Logan's glowed,
And there beside a swamp he drew,
O'er which dense mass of cedars grew.
Which cast around as drear a shade
As e'er at night a forest made;
Where hooting owls at times were heard.
And reptiles that amidst it stirred;
From whence black bats by thousands flew.
Mosquitos huge as ever grew,
And hawks revealed themselves to view,
As dismal shrieks on air they threw;
That swamp a gloomy look displayed
As ever man at night surveyed;
At night or day but few were known
Who by it cared to go alone;

The peasants all that country round,
Declared that it was haunted ground ;
All who at night had by it been
Had strange, unearthly marvels seen ;
Shapes that had filled their souls with awe,
Scenes far surpassing nature's law ;
Heard mysterious noises there
Which made the bravest quake with fear ;
Many declared strange lights they'd seen
At night, glow in that forest green,
And seen unearthly figures glide
Around, and strive those lights to hide.
Many at midnight had espied
Fierce shapes on snorting horses ride
O'er heads of trees that forest round,
Whose hoof-falls gave a noisy sound,
As if they trod on frozen ground ;
Some seen enormous serpents rise
With flaming tongue and flashing eyes,
High o'er the heads of tallest trees,
And hiss unto the midnight breeze ;
Some seen terrific spectres stride
From bough to bough, that forest wide,
While streamed from fleshless limbs the
    blood,
That dyed the forest with its flood ;
Some, murdered babes and mothers seen,
In air rise from that forest green ;
Had seen their gore terrific stream,
And heard both babes' and mothers'
    scream.
And countless tales like these were told
About this place by young and old ;
All said they felt a sense of awe
Whenever near the place they'd draw,
And often had the peasants round

Set fire to this haunted ground,
But each declared it would not burn,
That something back the flames would turn,
That they would only flicker there
A moment's space, then disappear,
Though in dry weather there they past,
And midst foliage dense and vast
The flaming brands with care they cast
While on them blew the sultry blast;
Yet by fire it was not harmed,
Against the force of flame 'twas charmed.

XVIII.

If Crawford Storm had e'er believed
The tales men of this place conceived,
His mind with hate was too much fraught
To give them then one passing thought,
For deadly vengeance filled his soul
And swayed it with its fierce control.
Had horrid shape, or spectre dread
Before him from that thicket sped,
Instead of filling him with fear,
He would have gladly halted there—
Hhailed it as a glorious sight,
And welcomed it with fell delight—
Had strove to learn the surest way
To give his deadly vengeance sway;
But neither ghoul nor goblin grim
Of giant form nor horrid limb,
If such there were, could frighten him, ·
For he was cruel, bold and brave,
As ever breathed, or filled a grave.

XIX.

On, on his snorting courser flew—
Had half-way by the thicket drew,
When, sudden to his horses head,
A figure from the thicket sped.
" Halt! Halt! " a voice abruptly cried,
While at the reins a hand did glide,
And just as sudden flashed in air
From out the woods, a pistol's blare,
While, hissing over man and horse,
In air a bullet found its course;
And far away that pistol's sound
Re-echoed o'er that thicket round;
The startled steed leapt high in air.
Neighed loud as was that pistol's blare;
But not one sign of dastard fear
Did Crawford's haughty features wear.
'Twas well for him who stopped his steed
That Crawford was of weapons freed,
For had he such at his command
His rein had never felt that hand;
Nor swifter shot nor surer aim,
Could any more than Crawford claim;
Oft had he proved that virtue well,
In many a duel, dread and fell,
For ne'er a foe before him came
But felt his sure and fatal aim.

XX.

" Had I a pistol," calm he said,
" I long ere this had stretched you dead!
Of weapons I am not bereft—
Entirely defenseless left,

So, ruffian, do not dare to stay
My steed, nor bar at all my way."
Swift, as he speaks, a dagger sheen
Down flashing, in his grasp is seen,
And almost strikes the burly hand
Of him who by his horse doth stand;
'Twas well that hand the bridle left,
Else Crawford's dagger it had cleft.
The while this passed, a ruddy glare
From whence had come that pistol's blare
Shone from a lantern dazzling bright,
Which far and wide cast round its light.
Right full on Crawford's face it glowed,
And all his haughty visage showed;
Then straight a surly voice was heard
That from the dismal thicket stirred,
" Ryan, set that wanderer free,
He's not our man, I plainly see;
Damn the luck, that to-night we find!
Mosquitos me have bitten blind;
Let's out of this infernal place,
For sooner hell itself, I'd face,
Than linger here a moment more,
And thus be bitten blind and sore!

XXI.

The light that from the lantern glowed
Soon unto Crawford's vision showed
The man who'd from the thicket sped
And who had seized his horse's head,
Was some officer of the law,
Plain on his breast its badge he saw.
Soon as this fact his eye espied,
" Who seek ye here?" he hoarsely cried,

"If not a secret, tell it me,
I may to you some service be;
For well I know this country round,
And every man that's in it found."
As thus he spake, from out the wood
Three men came forth and near him stood.

XXII.

All too wily, cunning, deep and sly,
Filled with craftiness of basest dye,
Are all such men, who fill the sphere
Of those that Crawford spake to there,
To ever make their secrets known
Save unto spirits like their own;
And this, at times they only do,
In hopes to gain some secret clue
Will help to drive their business through,
And aid them win the offered spoil
Which amply will reward their toil;
And 'twere not for the shining hoard
That always doth their toil reward,
No fear such men would ever chase
An outlaw to his hiding place;
And often such from them go free
If they can pay the largest fee;
Of all such men this will be found
A gospel truth the world around.
Such are all servants of the law
That ever yet dame nature saw;
Take on the bench the highest Judge,
Unto his lowest, meanest drudge,
Or purest of the lawyer crew
Who e'er breath in a forum drew,
None care how outlaws statutes foil,

If they will with them share their spoil;
Whoever pays the largest fee
Will in the end the victor be;
The innocent may pine and bleed,
They care not, so they win their meed;
And this holds good unto the crew
That sometimes on the streets we view,
There loafing with a club and star,
Or swilling grog at tavern bar.

XXIV.

But no detectives ever yet
A slyer man than Crawford, met,
For a detective, too, was he,
A lawyer, too, of high degree,
And ere they could suspect his drift
He would their secrets solve and sift;
Yea, draw out every secret there
Ere aware of the fact they were;
And soon he learned from them the cause
Why there they made his journey pause:
"Now," said the foremost of those men,
" You do all our errand ken,
Say, can you give us any clue
Will lead to him we now pursue?
If so, 'twill to your good accrue."
" I cannot," Crawford swift replied;
" 'Tis long since I have him espied;
Perhaps three fleeting months have pass'd
Since I on Ragan looked my last;
But, now, I would not think it strange,
If he were found at Logan's grange;
This night it chanced I took a road
Which brought me close to that abode:

Bright lights in every window glowed,
And merry throngs the porches showed;
To-night there's frolic, there, I trow,
And there you'll surely find him now.
No frolic yet that mansion knew,
But 'mongst its guests you'd Ragan view;
For, with old Logan he's in league,
Knows all his cunning and intrigue,
And if he has this murder done,
As sure as there is moon and sun,
We'll learn, when comes the proper time,
Logan was privy to the crime."
But stay; I will for you, turn back,
And you can follow on my track;
Right straight to Logan's I will go,
And if he's there, you'll shortly know.
"Be this the sign;—If he is there,
I will not back to you repair,
But in the mansion will remain,
If not, we'll shortly meet again;
And should we meet in Logan's hall,
Me do not recognize at all;
For I'd not have it known 'twas me
Who brought you to disturb their glee."

XXV.

He turned his steed, and forth he sped,
Fleet as e'er cloud on tempest fled;
The four within a clumsy wain,
On, on sped after him amain;
In vain, in vain they urge their steeds,
Too swift for them fierce Crawford leads;
And long ere they had driven more
Than half their dreary journey o'er,

The stately form of Crawford strode
Within old Logan's bright abode—
With beaming brow and smiling face,
Amidst the frolic took his place;
Midst all that mirth and festive scene,
Than him none wore a gayer mien.

XXVI.

O'er dreary roads, on, on amain,
With those four sped, the clumsy wain,
With oaths and lash they urge their steeds,
But soon lose sight of him who leads;
So rough and long the road they found,
They made the air with oaths resound.
"Ryan," said one, "I do believe
That us that scoundrel doth deceive;
And it has dawned upon my mind
That Logan's we will never find;
But then, we'd better forward move,
And straight his truth or falsehood prove,
However rough the road may grow,
Than ever deign to backward go
To yonder hellish swamp below."
"Yes," said Ryan, "we will proceed,
Long as we have a living steed;
Methinks that man I've seen before,
Some years ago—it can't be more
Than eight years back, or half a score;
Yes, him a dozen times, I ween,
I've pleading in the forum seen."
"I think he's kin unto the Judge,
Upon whose warrant now we drudge,
And on whose warrants oft we trudge,
And does us ample pay begrudge."

" Then," said the first, " if this be so
He will to Logan's mansion go ;
And then the least he'll do, I trow,
Tell Ragan we are coming now ;
And if the villain don't take flight
And cheat us of our prey to-night,
He will astonish me outright."
" He may have gone," another said,
" If he is poor and shrewd of head
And knows the value of a dime,
To post Earl Ragan that his crime
Has come to light, and he is sought
To answer for the deed he wrought ;
And straight forth make the fool engage
Him his defence in court to wage ;
I trust he'll win an ample fee—
But not a mite of it we'll see ;
Though through us he'll his client win
He will be just as mean as sin,
Nor share with us one single dime,
Though we posted him in time ;
And not a mite of it he'd won
Had we not told him what was done."
" And," said another, " if Judge Down
Is kin unto that slim-built clown,
You bet upon your life, your head
Earl Ragan will be richly bled—
Made to shell out an ample fee,
So he may of this crime pass free.
But those twain will keep it all,
No mite of it to us will fall ;
And when they've proved him void of guilt,
That 'twas not him this life-blood spilt,
Then we shall win no glowing spoil
To pay us for this night of toil.

And this will be the end, I trow,
As sure as I am speaking now.
I wish, if 'twere but for one year,
I had the sway of Down's chair,
I, too, would win huge, glowing piles,
Like those on which he often smiles."

XXVII.

While thus they spoke with thoughts that
          burned
And hearts that after treasure yearned,
To'rds the right the road abruptly turn'd
Up steeper and far higher ground,
But as with oath and curse, around
This rough and narrow curve they wound,
Themselves at Logan's home they found;
Swift from their clumsy wain they drew,
And through the windows cast their view:
Loud were the sounds of joy within,
Mixed with sweet music's sprightly din;—
The dance was set, and old and young
Were seen those joyous sets among.
" It is a sin," grim Ryan said,
A gloom 'mongst such a throng to spread,
Each vision looks as happy there,
As though Sorrow never trod this sphere;
And yon broad youth with sandy hair,
Although he wears an honest air—
Has frank and open face and brow,
Is him that we are after now.
I swear he does not look to me
One who might a murderer be !
But by looks we can't always tell,
'Neath heaven may be hid a hell ! "
This said, he trod the porch's floor,
And roughly knocked upon the door.

XXVIII.

'Twas Logan's hand that open flung
The door on which that knock had rung,
And scarcely was it open thrown
Than Ryan said, in harsh, hoarse tone,
" If Ragan's 'mongst those dancers there.
Tell him that he is wanted here."
But scarcely had been breathed his name,
Than to the door Earl Ragan came,
Then swift towards him grim Ryan made.
His hand upon his shoulder laid,
And " Sir, you are my prisoner ! " cried
With voice that sounded far and wide.
" Prisoner ! For what crime ? " Ragan said.
" In seizing me, you are misled."
" ' Is not ' Earl Ragan ' your right name ? ' "
" It is." " Then 'twas for you I came.
Just please to follow me along,
Or feel the weight of fetters strong."
" Then show your warrant.   For what
          crime
Am I arrested at this time ? "
" The warrant I can show, but trow
'Tis useless wasting moments now ;
For far, indeed, have we to wend
Ere we shall reach the journey's end."
" Then tell me for what crime I'm ta'en,
Now make to me that knowledge plain,
I have a right the cause to know."
" Then I will straight the warrant show,
But guess you know the cause full well,
And to you scarcely need it tell.

It is for murder."   At the word
A heavy groan from Logan stirr'd
Which was through all his mansion heard,
And on the floor fell as the dead,
While deathly hue his vision spread.
A flaky foam his lips o'ercast,
And seemed all life had from him past.

XXIX.

Earl Ragan stood bewildered deep,
As one half roused from troubled sleep.
While thus he stood, bound on his hands
Were clanking chains with brazen bands,
And swift unto the far-off wain,
Was carried by those men amain ;
And soon adown the road it sped,
While roared the driver's curses dread ;
The mirth was hushed, and every soul
Seemed everwhelmed with leaden dole.
Unto her sire Mary flew
Soon as his awful fate she knew ;
And round their host the guests all sped
With terror and with sorrow dread.
Deep sadness fell on every soul,
And all the joy thus turned to dole.
Another form had fled from there,
But when he went and unto where,
No one could any judgment form ;
That other one was Crawford Storm.

PART II.

I.

Amid this world some hearts are found
Without one charm of pity crowned,
Yea, ruthless as the granite stone
That is in caves of ocean thrown;
Or marble slab that lines the tomb,
And rests amid eternal gloom;
Cold as the barren rocks that show
Their peaks mid everlasting snow;
Where only icy breezes blow,
And summer suns shall never glow;
Which ne'er shall fruit nor vintage know,
But night its shadows o'er them throw;
And thus shall dwell in gloom and rime,
Until shall come the end of time,
When God shall wreck all nature's frame
And wrap it in destroying flame;
Those barren rocks to atoms burn,
Or to some other substance turn;
And from the wreck of ruin warm,
From amidst the fiery storm,
A fairer world of earth shall form—
Bring her from the fiery roar,
A blooming world forevermore;
Whose surface never spot shall show
On which fair vintage cannot grow;
No barren spot again shall know,
But all like rose and lily blow;
Yea, beauty shall caress the whole
And vintage bloom from pole to pole;
No useless, barren spot be found,
However small creation round.

So shall all souls of human kind
That ever God to flesh consigned,
Who unto others' woes are blind,
Nor e'er let pity sway their mind;
Whose spirits never yet were fraught
With one ray of generous thought
For any form of flesh and bone,
Save for their selfish selves alone—
Fiends who rejoice o'er others' woes,
Wretches who smile at others' throes,
And as through life they take their course
They never feel the least remorse
For any wrong they caused their kind,
Though they all basely it designed;
Wrought it midst all their hopes and fears;
Premeditated it for years;
Cold, barren hearts that never knew
One thought to noble nature true;
Spirits whom God has from the first,
With selfishness and envy curst;
And has but placed them here on earth—
Within this world let them have birth,
To show the rest of humankind
Out of what stuff is hell designed;
Spirits with passion ever hot,
And would foul murder do, if not
For terror of the hangman's cord,
And joyous noise such deed abroad;
Foul wretches who would lead astray
Those innocent as buds of May,
And gloat with joy o'er all their course
Without one feeling of remorse.
Oh, shortly may the time arrive,
Such souls in whelming hell shall strive;

And be to woe forever hurled,
Their natures crushed from off the world!
Be driven far from nature's shore
And never blight her regions more;
Be freed of every curse and doom
And in her pristine glory bloom;
May peace and joy pervade her shore
From pole to pole forevermore;
Goodwill and love 'mongst humankind
Be only to her realm consigned;
Make war and woe and famine cease,
And all that tends to rupture, peace;
And may the just and righteous Lord
Cast knowledge o'er her surface broad,
To every creed and hue and race
That breathe upon her blooming face;
Make every earth-born spirit tend
To Him their Father, Guide and Friend—
Their sole Beginning and their End,
To Him may all their feeling wend;
To all, of high or low degree,
Pour down His knowledge kind and free,
Till filled with it all earth shall be,
As do the waters fill the sea.

II.

And Crawford Storm was such a mind
As is to every virtue blind;
Would deal on others lasting woe,
And, fiend-like, laugh at every throe;
A cruel wretch with heart of stone,
Who lived but for himself alone.
Wild was the mirth his spirit knew
As he from Logan's mansion drew;

One look askance with joy he cast
As he by senseless Logan passed,
And saw the dole he well could trace
There plainly limned on Mary's face;
And saw the clanking chains and bands,
Those ruffians placed on Ragans hands;
There wild commotion reigned so high
None saw him as he passed them by
Noiseless as ever zephyr blew,
He swift from out that mansion drew;
Far down a winding path he passed,
And soon himself in saddle cast;
Then swift away his courser sped
On road that up the mountains lead
With foamy bit and flying mane
Darker than ever cloud became,
And spurs dyed o'er with gory stain
That steed with rider passed amain;
O'er narrow roads that darkly wound
By deep defile and rocky ground,
By thickets dense and deep morass
Which few by day could safely pass;
For through those wilds no roadway drew.
But well that steed and rider knew;
And seemed that steed as void of fear
As was the wretch who spurred him there;
For at no object e'er he shied
He on the gloomy road espied,
Though o'er his path from thickets round
Some startled deer would often bound,
Or goats, with long and flowing beard,
That thickly in those wilds were reared.

III.

As through the gloom fierce Crawford went
O'er deep defile and rocky bent,
His thoughts in speech found often vent,
And words like these on air he sent :—
" Yes, yes, what I to-night have seen,
Doth all my soul from sorrow wean,
And I rejoice o'er what is done
Far more than had I treasure won ;
Yea, as huge a pile as ever glowed,
Or e'er old Crœsus' coffers showed ;
Oh, it is more than joy supreme,
Thus sure to carry out one's scheme !
Before to-morrow's sun shall set
That fool in prison cell shall fret ;
For murder I will have him tried,
Nor shall conviction be denied ;
He from the gallows shall be swung
As sure as e'er was mortal hung,
Though scarce a living soul shall know
"Twas I who caused his overthrow ;
And I will teach that haughty maid
All homage must to me be paid ;
For when she is of Ragan free,
None other love but me she'll see ;
Than him, me she shall love far more,
Yes, yes, my very name adore ;
I know just how her soul to charm :
Distrust of me I shall disarm ;
In me she'll never dream of harm
As to my breast I draw her form
And on her plant my kisses warm ;

She'll love me with a deathless flame,
Although I can't return the same ;
For love to me is all unknown,
Its germs in me were never sown ;
When Nature cast me in her mould
Perhaps she let those germs grow cold,
Ere them amidst the rest she threw,
And with the rest they never grew ;
Or else perhaps she did forgo
One germ amidst the mass to throw,
So I might proudly stand above
That tainted thing, called Human Love ;
And look down on my dupes below,
Who that passion did on me bestow.

                              V.

Oh, what a kindling joy I felt,
As o'er her father's form she knelt !
I saw her eyelids bathed in tears,
And saw her features' ashen fears,
As propping up that father's head ;—
I only hope that he is dead.
If it be so, then none at all
Will bar me from her coming fall.

                             VI.

As thus he speaks, he reached a bield
That stood 'mongst scrub-wood well con-
        cealed,
Within a deep, but narrow vale ;
A light, but flickering and pale,
Shone out through one small, narrow pane
Where mud and filth made ample stain,

And was the only window there,
Round all that shanty dark and drear.
On earth leapt Crawford, swift and free,
And tied his courser to a tree,
And nimble as a deer he strode
Unto that dismal small abode ;
But on that door no hand he laid,
Nor any knock at all he made,
But on the wall touched a secret spring,
And straight inside a bell did ring.
Scarce was that low, dull larum sprung,
Within those log and mud walls rung,
Than bolts inside were backward swung,
And straight the door was open flung :
" Good morning, Boss ; " a voice was
  heard
To say, in low and whispered word,
As Crawford crossed that threshold o'er,
And trod upon that shanty's floor.

VII.

Him who the door had open thrown
And through the gloom was dimly shown,
Had thus accosted Crawford Storm,
Was a man of short and brawny form.
His strong arms all plain appeared,
Up to his very shoulders bared,
For all of sleeves his shirt was shorn—
Showed plain from where they had been
 · torn ;
The filthy robe his shoulders drest
Through rents showed plain his swelling
  breast ;

And all the garments that he wore
Huge signs of rents and patches bore ;
The patched-up shoes by him were worn,
To wear might any beggar scorn.
However poor and vile he be,
Degraded to the last degree.
From his white hair and grizzly beard,
Advanced in years, that man appeared ;
His locks, pale as the purest snow,
Hung heavy o'er his forehead low—
Almost his sluggish eyes concealed.
Which none of sprightly ray revealed ;
Whate'er had been their hue of old,
When he was young, could not be told.
For they had lost their primal shade.
Whate'er that hue had Nature made,
Through the foul grog he amply used,
With which he much his strength abused.
His daily drink had changed their hue—
Of primal shade left not a clue,
And made them look like balls of blood
That move around in milky flood ;
And more, their change had been provoked
By noxious pipe he ever smoked.
And well his huge, round, Roman nose
Did frequent use of grog disclose.
So dense o'er all his face appeared
His shaggy, matted, grizzly beard,
It all completely hid its lair,
Nor showed that visage of despair.
Though swiftly by him Crawford past
By breath that from his mouth he cast
Right plain could Crawford tell, and see
That he had just been drinking free ;

Though well, the pipe his mouth revealed,
The reeking fumes of grog concealed.
But little Crawford cared for this,
Nor e'er his drinking deemed amiss—
So him he aided heart and hand
To carry out the schemes he planned.
And such old Bolton well performed
If well his soul with grog was warmed;
From none of Crawford's tasks he swerved
If flaming grog his spirit nerved.

VIII.

" Pardon me, Bolton," Crawford spake,
" Maybe I did your slumbers break ;
But it is mainly for your sake
That I, myself, am now awake,
By all the saints, in bliss, I vow !
So please excuse my presence now.
Winter, you know, is coming fast,
With all its snow and icy blast,
And time, it is, to straight prepare
To gather in that season's cheer ;
And by this time, old friend, I trow
Your barrel is nigh empty now ;
So I propose to have it filled
With the best whiskey now distilled.
Ere goes a week I'll have it here,
And safely lodged beneath your care ;
And your tobacco stock, also,
By this must be extremely low,
Your bags with it must soon be stored,
The best the market can afford."

IX.

"Thank you, Boss Crawford," Bolton said,
" My stock of each has almost fled ;
Please give to me your order now,
And if the grace of God allow,
This very day I'll go to town
And bring my stock for winter down."
" I will to you the order give,
And you'll this winter jolly live
As any man within the land,
Though he have wealth at his command."
Thus Crawford having spoke, he took
From out his coat a little book,
Right swift he did it open throw
And on a page as white as snow
That order wrote in letters bold,
Tore off the page, and did it fold,
Around it tied a silken band
And gave it unto Bolton's hand,
Saying, " Old friend, one cask, I trow,
Will scarcely last from Spring till'now,
So I herein have ordered three,
And quality of best degree :
Also, just twenty extra pounds
Of tobacco, cut and dried ; " Zounds ! "
Old Bolton hoarsely cried in glee,
" I thank you for your bounty free,
May such generous souls as yours
Win all bliss that Heaven procures ;
From this henceforth, I swear my hand
Shall do whatever you command,
As in the past it's always done,
And never sought a task to shun

However hard it seemed to be,
And none of mortal perils free ;
God bless your soul, forevermore ! "
Muttered old Bolton o'er and o'er.

X.

A smile o'er Crawford's features ran,
Which did his haughty visage span
As he surveyed that hoary man,
And thus to him his speech began :
" I swear by all the saints above,
Who live in harmony and love,
That it doth make my inmost soul
With seething tide of rapture roll
To witness joy like yours, and know
I did the cause of joy bestow !
To do a good to human kind,
It doth delight me, soul and mind.
In doing good I've spent my days
Since ever I controll'd my ways.
But say ! my dear old friend, just now,
If I did right your meaning trow,
You said you'd gladly do for me
Whate'er my wishes might decree ?
If I have guessed your meaning right
I'll tell you of a scheme to-night
That I would like you do for me
Before a week from now shall flee,
Nor is it half as hard to do
As have right oft been done by you."

XI.

" Let's hear it." Bolton swift replied,
And closer drew to Crawford's side.

" Dear Boss, you know that any deed
I'd do for you, nor ask the least of meed;
Say, did not I with my own hand,
George Musgrave slay at your command ?
The simple fool I led astray
Where often Ragan bent his way,
Where seldom others chanced to pass,
And crushed him to a shapeless mass ;
His bloody clothes I off him drew,
His body in a whirlpool threw,
From whence 'twill never rise to view,
Then swift to Ragan's barn I drew
And did them there all careless hide,
Red with the gore of Musgrave dyed—
Did all as I with you agreed
When for the task you paid the meed,
And as you wished, I took good heed—
Although I did the job with speed—
To do it so all men 'twould lead
To fancy Ragan did the deed :
Yea, throw on him all taint of crime,
And this you'll see, in course of time.
And now, whate'er you wish of me,
I care not what your will decree,
I'll do it for you just as free
As comes the air to grass or tree."

XII.

" I believe you would," the other said,
" Think you would risk your life, your head,
And hail your death with joy supreme,
If but to carry out my scheme
Should be your sole reward. Far more
You I like, than do I Hugh Lenore.

" I like not to divulge my thought
To those weak souls who with love are
    fraught,
Or in the snares of women caught,
Nor have my secret schemings wrought
By a man who love for woman feels,
And ever has one at his heels;
The time will come, howe'er delayed,
When everything will be betrayed
When once a woman knows a tale;—
She'll noise it o'er hill and dale;
And men, alas, are all too frail,
Too oft their thoughts to them unveil
For me to risk my limb or life
By him who has what's called a wife;
So as you do not have one here,
Nor deign to claim one anywhere,
I do not fear to trust with you
The greatest scheme I wish to do.
I know you would no secret tell
No matter what the scheme befell,
But hide it in you just as well
As doth your heart within you dwell,
That drives through all your form the
    blood,
And ever active keeps that flood.
No, no, it would more hidden be
Than is the heart in you or me,
For it will flutter, thump and beat,
The sense of sound it cannot cheat,
And plainly unto it doth prove
That something in the breast doth move;
No, far more secret must it be,
Like thing we cannot hear nor see,
As stone in ocean's deepest flow,
That ne'er itself to man will show.

XIII.

"Yes, Boss," the other said, "you know,
Betide me weal, betide me woe,
I would not e'er your schemes reveal
Though sorest wound of mine 'twould heal;
And though pierced through with burning
    steel
I would your schemes from all conceal.
No fear of me; go on and tell
Just how I can aid you now." "Well
You are the man, old boy, for me,
And what I want you'll shortly see.
See, did I say, I mean your ear
Shall swiftly all my projects hear?
There is a maid I wish to snare,
And crave that you the deed will dare;
Within a week I wish her caught,
And here within this shanty brought;
You find the aid to do this deed,
And I will pay most ample meed;
I trust 'tis vain for me to lay
A plan to guide you on your way;
In such tasks far too well you're skill'd,
To e'er by me be trained or drill'd.
Now say, will you do this for me?
I swear I'll pay most ample fee!"
"Yes; I will do it, just as sure
As heaven seems an azure pure,
Though ne'er a mite for it be paid;
But say, where is, and who the maid?"
"'Tis Mary Logan." "By my soul!
Betide it weal, betide it dole,
Before a week she shall be caught,
And for you to this shanty brought;

The task I would for you perform
Were gratitude but half as warm,
But this doth all my being swarm ! "

XIV.

As Bolton spake, proud Crawford Storm,
With haughty features wreathed in smile.
Gazed in these sluggish eyes the while,
There thought he saw no hidden guile,
Nor craftiness of any style ;
And as the old man ceased, he said,
" Give me your hand ; when next I tread
Upon this shanty's floor, old boy,
We'll have enough of cause for joy ;
With pleasure shall all hearts be crown'd
If here by me that maid be found,
Which none of earthly words can tell,
So adieu, till then." " Yes, farewell,"
The old man said, and tightly grasped
The hand that round his own was clasp'd,
And hoarsely said " farewell again,
And if to capture her be vain,
Then parted may we aye remain,
Nor ever meet in joy or pain."
" Yes, be it so," the other cried,
And swiftly left the old man's side ;
Then quick the door he opened wide
And to'rds his steed did lightly glide ;
The reins within his hand he drew,
Himself within the saddle threw
And back upon the road again,
His courser went with flying mane.
By this, o'er skies a feeble ray
From out the east began to play,

Which sends the heralds on their way
To tell the earth 'tis coming day.

XV.

Scarce had the haughty Crawford rode
From sight of Bolton's drear abode,
Than into it two figures strode
With sacks filled with some weighty load,
And as they did each heavy sack
Upon that shanty's floor unpack,
They proved to be a mingled spoil
Of flour, hams and cans of oil,
Sugar and rice, and things I trow,
To tell were long and needless now,
Suffice it this, all there they bore,
They'd stolen from a distant store,
Whose owner on that very night
Was mingling with the gay delight
Which all the while at Logan's past
Until it was with gloom o'ercast—
Till on it fell that sudden blast
Which made it cease in sorrow vast.

XVI.

Of all unsightly, beastly men,
Who ever roamed o'er moor or fen,
On mountain, or through lonely glen,
Or ever pined in prison den—
Or ever trod on vessel's deck,
Or on the gallows stretched their neck—
None more debased in soul and form
Have ever trod in shine or storm,
Than were those two unsightly men
Who came in Bolton's dismal den,

Who, soon as he beheld the spoil,
With grog rewarded well their toil;
And unto each he dealt his fill—
One he styled " Joe," the other " Bill ; "
The first was tall of form, and spare,
With grizzly beard and grayish hair,
Whose face all o'er was seam'd and scarr'd,
Which much his visage damn'd and marr'd;
One eye was gone—lost years ago
In combat with some deadly foe,
Who also in that fearful close
Had bitten off both ears and nose,
And bitten from his hairy lip
So ghastly and so large a strip
The grizzly hair those parts reveal'd
But scantily its loss conceal'd,
And showed all plainly there beneath,
That horrid mouth of broken teeth.
The other was a shorter man,
A model of far different plan,
And, judging by his sable hairs,
Far younger by a score of years ;
And dark his eyes as coals that 'shine
'Neath lantern's rays in gloomy mine ;
His sable hair but ill supplied
The roughness of his skin to hide,
Where horrid small-pox years before
Had left unsightly seams he wore ;
But other scars he also bore,
Ta'en in many a fray of yore,
While his rough lips that showed no hair,
And thick as ever mortal's were,
Did all a strong resemblance bear
To looks that nutmeg graters wear ;

Within one leg the wretch was lamed,
Also in other parts was maimed.
Perhaps if these two wretched men
Had not been found in Bolton's den,
But in a nobler sphere of life,
Crowned with hideousness so rife
They'd not seemed so to mortal eye
That carelessly had passed them by;
But found in such a den of crime,
They seem'd the foulest fiends of time
That ever breathed this vital air
Or peopled dens of dread despair.

XVII.

This was the all inhuman aid
With whom his plans old Bolton laid,
To bring through craft, or wile or raid,
Mary, that all transcendant maid,
A captive to his dismal bield,
And her unto vile Crawford yield.
After his plans with them he'd laid
And fixed the day to trap the maid,
" Now boys," said he, " To-day I go
My order to the grocer show,
And ere the sunset embers burn
I will with all my grog return,
With boxes of tobacco, too,
So we'll have lots to smoke and chew ;
And grog we'll have this winter, drear,
So time away shall jolly wear ;
Yea, I'll come back with as fair a load
As ever yet my wagon showed ;
Oh, jolly times are coming, boys !
Let winter tempests make their noise,

We shall have our share of joys,
For we will have our cherished toys—
'Bacco and grog! what need we more,
When nights are long and winter hoar?
To here no man will us pursue,
No matter what we dare to do—
So 'gainst Judge Down we do no deed
No other one have we to heed,
For he owns all these mountains broad—
No doubt he won them all by fraud,
And if he did, I like him more
Than though he'd paid in yellow ore,
For then less likely he is to chide
My deeds, but help me them to hide—
Teach those by whom they are espied—
To view them on their sunny side.
Full many deeds I've done for him,
Which savored of the dread and grim—
Deeds for which better men than I
Have oft and oft been doomed to die,
Yes, from the horrid gibbet swung,
Or been for life in dungeon flung.
And when for any deed I wrought
Old Bolton was to trial brought,
(For I own in some I have been caught)
All, all against me came to naught,
Down freed me of each fearful charge
And straight again set me at large.
In court, to many a lie I've sworn
At his command, and did not scorn
To go for him at any time
He wished me to perform some crime ;
So, to reward me for my deeds,
And provide for my daily needs,

He placed me here within this home
And gave me all these hills to roam;
Placed everything beneath my care—
Those forests with their goat and deer,
And all the people, far and near,
Are too afraid to venture here,
Lest unto Down I should it tell
They hunted o'er his hill and dell,
And kill'd his game—quail, goats, and deer.
They know if such report he'd hear
He would to them no mercy show,
But would them straight in dungeons
    throw,
On sand and water have them fed,
Instead of luscious grog and bread;
So, boys, we have no cause to fear
That anyone will venture near,
That would to us defiance show,
Or on us least of insult throw;
Or at our grimest deed dare frown;
Crawford is nephew to Judge Down,
And we must help his kith and kin
All wishes of their souls to win,
Nor reck not should their tasks be grim;
So we that bird must cage for him,
And if it can't through gentle course
Be done, it must be wrought through
    force."

XVIII.

As o'er their whiskey planning crime
These ruthless wretches pass their time,
With spirit with grim malice warm,
O'er dale and hill rode Crawford Storm;

Till Logan's mansion met his view,
Till there himself from saddle threw,
There once more o'er that threshold drew,
Which from that day no more his presence
    knew.
With light, elastic, nimble tread,
He through the winding hallway sped,
Soon to a spacious room he wound,
And there the maid and father found;
He greeted each with friendly air,
And by the old man drew his chair.
It seemed o'er John Logan's face
Despair had made its resting place,
So grimly grief sat on his brow,
E'en Crawford scarcely knew him now;
One shock from palsy's ghastly blow,
Had made his eyes unearthly glow;
Their pure bright azure sheen had changed
And left it strangely disarranged;
So altered was that old man's mien
From what till then was always seen.
It seemed a score of years had fled,
And on him all their tempests shed
Of sorrows, troubles, gloom and blight,
Instead of one short fleeting night.

XIX.

With flaming joy did Crawford glow
To see the old man's look of woe,
But by no slightest sign he showed
The secret mirth that in him glowed;
Sad as a priest of gravest air,
He by John Logan took his chair;

He took in his the old man's hand
And spoke in accents meek and bland;
But all he said, on Mary's ear
Fell just as deadening and as drear
As do the winds of midnight gloom,
Sigh round the loved one's lonely tomb,
When o'er it bends the widowed soul,
Where hope no longer holds control,
And o'er the cold and voiceless dead
The last sad, burning tear is shed.

XX.

To repeat all Crawford spake, I trow,
Would be completely useless now,
Nor will the muse the time allow,
But all the while he spake, his brow,
His voice and visage, seemed the while
All free as is the air of guile.
He told John Logan o'er and o'er,
It grieved him so intensely sore
To be a witness of the plight
He'd seen him lying in last night
That he could not beside him stay,
So had abruptly sped away;
Yes, all too sensitive, he said,
Dame nature has his being bred,
To let him calmly stand by anyone
His love is strongly fixed upon,
And view their slightest throes of pain.
Said he, " my blood in every vein
Grows thick and cold as frozen snow—
Seems 'twill not through its channels flow,
And every bone and thew and nerve
Seems from its wonted use to swerve;

And none of aid his hand can lend,
Though 'twould straight ease his dearest
 friend."
Huge, briny tears, as this he told,
From his dark eyes abundant rolled,
Sped swiftly down his haughty face,
And, falling, reached the floor apace.

XXI.

Mary, as Crawford spake, the while
By neither look nor frown nor smile
Did sign of her disgust betray,
But looked as still and dead as clay.
He rose and gently left his chair,
Did to the maiden's side repair,
And with a sad but kindly look
Her hand within his own he took;
But it seemed soft and cold as snow
When first it falls to earth below,
And on the frozen leaf is thrown,
But pressure none save air has known;
A moment's space her eyes she raised,
Intensely into Crawford's gazed,
As though she there would ferret out
Something her senses yet would doubt,
Then turned her gaze a moment's space
Upon her father's sad, pale face;
Then swift from off her chair she flew.
Her form to its full height she drew,
Back from her brow her curls she threw,
On Crawford fixed her gaze anew,
The color from her visage fled
And left it paler than the dead,
Or than the frost on mountain's head,

But for a moment's space it sped,
Swift back again the bounding blood
Returned to it in crimson flood,
Again it swiftly ebbed away,
Left all her face more pale than clay.
While from her eyes shot forth a ray
Like glass when on it sunbeams play.
While heaved her breast like sea in storm,
And taller seemed to grow her form;
Thrice she essayed to speak, but thrice
Her tongue refused to move, like ice
Congealed midst vaults of lifeless stone,
It seem'd it in her mouth had grown.
At length it from its fetters broke,
And all bewildered thus she spoke:

XXII.

Avaunt! thou subtle, cruel fiend,
With soul of every virtue clean'd,
If e'er one on thy spirit lean'd
It has of it been ever wean'd!
Haste back to that infernal sphere
From whence thy spirit wandered here;
Go, bear it back from earth and time
Unto grim hell, its native clime,
Or to where'er that region be
Whence issued such a fiend as thee!
A wretch more treacherous than thou,
Has nature never seen till now,
And never while her seasons roll
Will time see more so vile a soul!
'Tis treacherous as ice that shows
Safe path 'neath which deep water flows.
That looks to hunters' eyes secure,
Whene'er they range from shore to shore,

On which they trusting tread, and feel
When all too late, the waters steal
Around their forms its icy flow,
And sudden meet in death below.
Thou couldst place poison in the cup,
And hold the deadly liquid up
For thy best friend on earth to drain,
Nor feel the least remorse nor pain!
Yea, think not, vile and subtle fiend,
I have not all your secrets gleaned.
That do your inmost thoughts control,
And pierced the chambers of thy soul!
The very thoughts that fill them now
I see as plainly as thy brow;
But think not any scheme of thine
Shall wholy injure me or mine.
Visions of prophecy I see—
An awful end they limn of thee;
After a life of darkest crime
As yet was ever known to time,
I see convulsed in form and limb,
Thee, dangling from the gallows grim.
I see thy schemes all come to naught,
And all the harm, for which thou wrought,
I see thy hate and vengeance dread,
Fall scatheless save on thy own head;
I see Earl Ragan pass unharmed,
As though he were by wizzard charm'd,
Through the hissing, fiery flame
Of blazing crime and burning shame,
All which thy cruel, evil soul
Wrought day and night on him to roll;
For God brought all thy schemes to naught
And thy own ruin with them wrought.

Repent, thou fiend, while yet it's time,
Turn from thy ways of subtle crime,
And show remorse for all thy sin ! "
Here Crawford on her speech broke in :
" Maiden, you know not what you say,
Methinks your reason much doth stray ;
Perhaps you are not now aware
Crime is on Ragan proven clear.
He basely shed George Musgrave's blood,
Then cast him in the whirlpool's flood ;
And there are witnesses, a score,
Who swear they saw him spill that gore,
Whose oaths, when comes the proper time,
Will prove on him this fearful crime ;
And e'en of this should he go free,
Which I fancy you will never see,
Still other charges hang o'er him
The law holds just as foul and grim ;
For forged unnumbered times has he,
All men he knew, their names used free.
Notes and checks written in his hand,
He's scattered thickly o'er the land,
And signed to these the names of men
Who'll fiercely punish him, I ken ;
And if he is not for murder hung,
He will for forgery be swung ;
So let your temper cool. young maid,
Of it is Crawford not afraid,
'Twas pity, simply, brought me here,
And this by all the saints, I swear,
I thought I might some service be
To people dearly loved by me,
For whom all that I have I'd give
If it would make them happy live,

Nor did I ever think to meet
Such strange reception as I greet;
But I forgive you all, young maid,
So fear not they'll be e'er repaid ;
Though harshly you do me upbraid
For laying snares that Ragan laid,
In which the proper victim fell,
I do forgive you just as well."

XXIII.

" Forgive ! " the maiden swift replied,
As fiercer flashed her eyes with pride ;
" I no forgiveness crave of you,
Nor would I ask it though 'twere due.
No, were I on the gallows grim,
And you could save my life or limb,
I'd sooner die the ghastly death—
Yea, gladly render up my breath—
Than think that I was saved the while,
By fiend like you, so low and vile!
Pardon from such a wretch as you,
That ne'er a noble feeling knew,
The meanest thing that crawls on earth—
That e'er in nature found its birth
Would scorn—despise to take your boon !
Your pity ! I would just as soon
It ask of some grim beast of prey
That prowls at midnight on its way
With hunger writhing all its form,
As ask such thing of Crawford Storm !
Haste, haste from here, you traitor vile,
The air we breathe no more defile ! "
Though fiercely thus she spake, he stood
Unruffled as a beam of wood,

Or statue all of iron cast;
No frown his haughty visage past,
But as she spake, o'er it the while,
There beamed a mild and lively smile;
By neither look nor sign nor word'
Betrayed the rage that in him stirred;
Nor his dark eyes with anger burned;
And as she ceased, he gently turned
His gaze upon her father's face,
Who, like a statue, kept his place,
And said to him with beaming smile,
"Hearest thou thy daughter me revile?
And dost thou think that I should meet
Such warm reception as I greet?—
And from the lips of one I love
All, far all breathing things above
As is the furthest star in space
Beyond this earth's cold, dismal face—
Whose love I fondly hoped to win?"
At this the father straight broke in :
"You have not heard me tell my child
Her speech was either rough nor wild,
And by this fact you well must see,
I with her thoughts and words agree;
And, Crawford, plain I tell you, now,
I know your soul belies your brow,
I see 'tis fill'd with anger dire,
But here you fear to show that ire.
Though hoar I am and fill'd with age,
No strife with me you'd dare to wage;
Though God this palsy on me sent
For some all-wise, divine intent,
And me of half my vigor shent,
It is not wholly from me rent,

And if you here your ire show,
Mark, I shall meet you blow for blow;
And if you rouse my anger more,
I swift will crush you to the floor."
Depart! you'll find the doorway there,
So do not longer tarry here."

XXV.

" If 'tis the wish of my old friend
That I should from his presence wend,
Then be it so; now I will go,
And, Logan, may all blessings flow,
Which gods to favored mortals show
Upon you and your lovely child.
When next we meet, I hope more mild
Will be your treatment unto me;
But when the time comes, this we'll see;
Give me your hand, and say adieu."
" No more I give my hand to you;
The adder's tongue I'd sooner feel
I crush to atoms 'neath my heel.
And one more truth, I tell you now,
If God will only me allow
The strength to mount upon my horse,
To-morrow I will take my course
Unto the jail, and Ragan see,
And from that dungeon set him free;
All lands I own shall be his bail;
If these won't free him of the jail,
Then I will bring my friends, around,
Who own vast fields of fertile ground;
Many, I know, who ne'er would fail
To aid me bail him out of jail.
And Crawford, mark, if you through vile
Malicious envy, craft or wile,

Have on Earl Ragan cast this crime,
You'll shortly find your reckoning time.
If men don't punish you for it,
And you should all the laws outwit,
His vengeance, God shall yet fulfill;
Linger, it may, but come it will;
Now, speed you hence upon your way,
I have no other word to say."

XXVI.

From Logan swiftly Crawford turned,
As though by bolt of lightning spurned,
And to'rds the spacious doorway sped
With form erect and haughty tread;
And saying as he crossed the floor,
" Farewell, dear friends, forevermore;
If these are thoughts you have of me—
Who am of all your charges free,
As is the infant yet unborn;
Although you do me treat with scorn.
To you I bear no evil thought,
And naught for you but kindness wrought."
Saying these words, he crossed the floor,
And swiftly gained the spacious door,
The threshold lightly passed he o'er,
Nor e'er cross'd that threshold more—
Parted like ships on stormy main,
That part and never meet again.

XXVII.

Swift on his steed his form he threw
And darted out of Logan's view
With spirit filled with rage and hate,
And frowning fierce on earth and fate,

He rode along at rapid rate
Until he reached that city's gate,
Wherein that dismal jail was found
Within whose walls was Ragan bound,
Fast up a broad and stately street
Thundered his chargers flying feet,
Until he reached a stately door
With steps of marble polished o'er,
The door huge plates of silver wore.
And these the name of owner bore ;
" Judge Down," on every plate was seen,
Graved all in grandest style, I ween.
A man met Crawford at the door,
Who office of a hostler bore,
Soon as of him was saddle freed,
That man to stable led his steed,
Swift o'er the threshold Crawford strode,
And soon was hid in that abode.

XXVIII.

Soon trod he to a spacious room
That gaudy curtains filled with gloom.
Curtains of damask, rich and rare,
Hung o'er those windows, placed with care,
Curtains of silken laces wrought,
With figures all superbly fraught
Shut out the light of glowing sun,
And fill'd that place with shadows dun ;
And o'er the floor were carpets seen
Of mingled shades of red and green.
Of scarlet, crimson, blue and gold,
And every color made or sold ;
Together these were choicely brought,
And richly were with figures wrought ;

Carpets as costly—well, I ween,
As ever yet were trod or seen
In stately court of proudest queen,
Whose eye for such was choice and keen;
Carpets as rich as ever loom
Wove for a monarch's grandest room—
All flowers seemed to o'er them bloom,
Though dimly seen amidst the gloom;
And all the furniture there seen,
Was of the grandest style, I ween,
The costliest that could be found
'Mongst all refindest nations round;
Every sofa, stool, lounge and chair
Was cushion'd o'er with velvet rare,
Wrought with flowers of every shade
And form, Dame Nature ever made,
As ever in her gardens bloom'd,
And grandest shapes and hues assumed.
With paintings all the walls were fraught,
Which had the greatest limners wrought
'Mongst all the nations, old and young,
And these from floor to ceiling hung;
Paintings of battles, fierce and wild,
Where slaughtered men in hills were piled,
Revealing rally, rout and charge—
The falling sword on helm and targe;
The broken shield, and blade and spear
The dying chief, the mourner's tear,
The features grim with rage or fear,
The smiles that haughty victors wear—
All limned in colors true to life,
Were teeming on the canvas rife;
Paintings of hurricane and storm,
Clouds torn with lightning red and warm,

With shapes of things the blasts deform,
Did o'er the life-like painting swarm;
Scenes of grim shipwrecks, and their woe,
Did there broad sheets of canvas show;
Limning of mountain lands sublime,
Of every wild, romantic clime,
Some robed in winter's garb of snow
Where roaring storms their fury show,
Where avalanches fall below
To vales where mighty torrents flow,
Where hills eternal shadows throw
And never signs of vintage know;
But where grim beasts enormous grow,
With teeth that gleam and eyes that glow,
And roar to storms with rage or woe
As couched on lairs of gore and slime
Amidst eternal blast and rime;
Some were decked in summer's prime,
And fair as ever known to time,
Yet all stupendous and sublime
As ever seen in nature's clime,
With flowers clad, and stately trees
That seemed to wave midst gentle breeze,
And on their sides of glowing green
Were flocks of sheep and shepherds seen:
Some landscapes gleam'd midst sunshine
    glow,
Some shone the moon's calm light below;
Some stood 'neath midnight's sable frown,
Nor star nor planet beaming down.
Besides these paintings, rich and rare,
That filled the walls and ceilings, there
Stood round that room some statues grand
As e'er were wrought by sculptor's hand.

XXIX.

Around this room his gaze he cast,
But amid all its splendor vast
No living creature met his view,
Swift to'rds another door he drew,
Across the threshold soon he past
And face to face met Down at last.

XXX.

The Judge sat at a spacious board
That with choice fare was amply stored,
With meat and fowl, and best of food,
The Judge supplied his hungry mood;
There sat the dishes, choice and rare
As ever made a monarch's fare;
The best of earth, or flood or air,
All nicely cooked was steaming there
On plates of solid silver bright,
That cast around their polished light;
And as he ate his throat he laved
With ruddy wine from cups engraved
With rare designs, devices strange
As ever yet did vision range;
Cups out of purest silver made,
And all with ruddy gold inlaid.

XXXI.

The Judge was short and thin of form,
Scarce half the height of Crawford Storm.
Shallow and narrow was his chest,
O'er which he wore a gaudy vest,
And there a golden pin he showed
That all with sparkling diamonds glowed.

And from his vest hung, plain to see,
Huge rows of seals that dangled free;
And all his garb from head to heel
Did perfect gaudiness reveal
His bony fingers also showed
Huge, weighty rings that flashed and
    glowed
With stones and gems of every shade
And hue that art or nature made.

XXXII.

Small was his form, and spare, I said—
Had o'er his length a rule been spread
And measured him from crown to floor,
Than four-feet-three, he'd proved no more:
And too enormous was his head,
Compared to what was 'neath it spread.
Broad and stupendous was its crown,
And towards its chin it tapered down;
It seem'd like some enormous pear—
Small to'rds the stem, but huge elsewhere.
Sure, at the time that head was wrought,
Dame Nature's mind must have been
    fraught
With model strange, and have caught
That of swift tapering retort;
For seldom e'er 'mongst men, I ween;
A head so queerly shaped was seen;
Modeled was it from chin to crown,
Like slanting hill turned upside down,
Forming a broad and heavy top,
With at its base too small a prop;
His wrinkled cheeks no whiskers wore,
Nor of these his chin an atom bore,

These parts were shaven smooth and clean.
But a heavy, gray mustache was seen,
Which, when moved his lips showed be-
    neath
White rows of artificial teeth ;
Down almost o'er his mouth there came
A warty nose of bulky frame,
Broad at its base, but at its end
'Twas sharp, and this did upward tend ;
His crown was bald as is the stone
On which ne'er moss nor grass was grown.
That is in bed of torrent seen,
And ne'er will grasses grow, I ween.
But halfway o'er that head, all round
Between the crown and ears, was found
A bushy growth of heavy hair,
Which gave to him an aged air ;
And 'neath his hoary eyebrows showed
His sable orbs that keenly glowed,
But plainly midst their flashing sheen
Deep, subtle craft and guile was seen.

XXXIII.

" God bless your soul, my darling boy ! "
Swift said Judge Down with seeming joy,
As o'er that threshold Crawford drew,
And came within his uncle's view.
" Now you have just arrived in time
To see Earl Ragan tried for crime—
Both forgery and murder grim ;
True bills have just been found 'gainst him;
I hurried through all things to-day,
And from him kept his friends away ;
To-morrow I shall have him tried—
More time to him shall be denied,

E'en should that boon be asked of me
By all his friends, who'er they be,
Although with broad dominions backed ;
I have the jury picked and packed,
And it will him convict just sure
As ever wine was red and pure,
And ever meant to moisten food
I swallowed in my hungry mood.
And when on him they fix the crime,
Then after that will come the time ;
It will be vain to offer bail,
Or hope to pledge him out of jail ;
When this is done, then you can woo
And marry Mary Logan too ;
Soon as that maiden is your wife,
Then try your hand at Logan's life—
Old men die easy ; then you reign
As master o'er his wide domain.
But then, remember one thing, boy,
If you would well your gain enjoy,
One-half the lands, you give to me ;
I claim them as my lawful fee.
Now, swear to me, when this is done—
When mastership o'er all you've won,
You, Crawford Storm, will not forget
To pay your uncle all this debt."
" Give me your hand, my uncle dear,
By all heaven and earth, I swear,
To you I'll leave no debt unpaid,
When once as wife I win that maid."

PART III.

I.

A long and dreary week had past,
Thick, murky clouds had skies o'ercast,
Cold rains to earth had fallen vast,
And ceaseless roared an autumn blast.
To trial had been Ragan brought,
And Down had his conviction wrought;
For men and women, full a score,
Whom Ragan ne'er had seen before—
Save two, of all that motley crew,
On him the crime of murder threw.
These two were Bolton and Lenore;
Each firmly and directly swore
That he had heard Earl Ragan swear
Three times, or more, within the year,
That he would take George Musgrave's life
With either rifle, club or knife;
But only one amongst them swore
That he had seen him shed that gore,
And that was him called Hugh Lenore.
He swore by church and holy rood,
That he had close beside him stood,
Had seen him deal on Musgrave's head
The fatal blow that stretched him dead;
Seen him disrobe the lifeless form
While yet the blood was streaming warm,
Saw him the naked body cast
Within a whirlpool fierce and vast,
From whence it never more shall rise
To show itself to human eyes.

" Yes," said he, true as holy writ,
Or, sure as here in court I sit,
I saw Earl Ragan, plain as now,
Take Musgrave's clothes unto his mow,
And there secrete them 'mongst the hay,
Just where we found them yesterday."

II.

When thus he swore, out spoke the Judge,
" Now, life, I do to no man grudge,
However low and vile he be,
And fallen, to the last degree;
I strive to let all ruffians live,
Nor take the boon I cannot give.
I often let them pass from here
With but a reprimand severe;
Many, perhaps, should have been hung,
Or for their lives in dungeon flung,
But through good heart, I let them go,
When their friends for them pleaded so.
But this I can no longer do,
Henceforth another course pursue;
Whoever now doth break the law,
And on himself its vengeance draw,
Must pay the cost for what he's done,
Although it be my only son;
I must in those who break the law,
Strike deep its terror and its awe.
Now, in this case I hope to see
The jury with their Judge agree,
And by their wise, august decree,
Not set this man of murder free.
Since I as Judge have ruled this place,
I never saw a plainer case

Of murder proven until now,
And hope the jury will allow—
Yea, give their verdict, swift and free,
Of murder in the first degree.
So go, my friends, and meditate,
On what shall be this ruffian's fate;
You see the crime on him is proved.

III.

As from their seats the jury moved
And pass'd unto a little room
To ponder over Ragan's doom,
Up from his seat the prisoner sprung,
And with a voice that loudly rung
Through all that spacious courtroom
    round,
Where, save it, was silence most profound.
Though it was crowded full of men,
With women and with children then;
And said to Down, " Most noble Judge,
I see you me of life begrudge;
But for this I do not care at all,
More than a rock heeds passing squall,
Which on its side can only bray,
Nor brings to it the least dismay;
A serpent's sting may strike a rock,
But it don't heed nor feel the shock;
The serpents jaws are only bruised,
Itself is all that is misused;
And you, too, yet will plainly see
Your venom all is lost on me;
The spleen you have on me diffused
This day, has only me amused;
I care not for it any more
Than granite does for storms that roar;

They only sweep the dust away
Cast there by time and grim decay,
Make them far brighter bodies show,
More in their pristine glory glow;
What I have seen and heard to-day
Smites me not with the least dismay;
It only serves to brush away
Dark ignorance that round me lay,
And kept my spirit grossly blind
Of characters in human kind,
But until now I never knew
There breathed on earth a fiend like you!
And had I heard this day's work told,
In any story, new or old,
I would have laid the book aside
And firmly thought the author lied.
Now, truth, I see, is far more strange—
More full of subtleness and change,
Than what is found in fiction's range,
However wild her flights she wield,
And shows her heart to pity steel'd;
Only one thing I cannot see,
But this may yet be shown to me
Ere ceases here on earth my time:
It is, why you this hellish crime
Have strove so hard to fix on me,
Who, well you know of it am free.
Yes, no more did the fearful crime
Than did yon clock, whose tick and chime
Knells on your ears the passing time;
Yes, of that dark and cruel deed,
You know full well that I am freed;
And there is not the slightest need
For me to say that I am free
Of charges you have brought 'gainst me."

As this he said, from out the room
Those twelve came forth to speak his doom ;
And grave as priests when mass they say,
Or round some lifeless sinners pray,
They formed a ring the prisoner round
Midst silence awful and profound,
Broke only by their footstep's tread,
And as they stood in silence dread,
A voice cried out in solemn tone,
" Now let it to the Court be known,
If you guilty or not guilty, find
The prisoner at the bar ? "   " One mind
Have we, the foreman swift replied,
About the guilt of him we've tried ;
And we pronounce he is not free
Of murder in the first degree !
No stronger proof we ever saw, ,
So now we give him to the law ! "

IV.

The while these words the foreman said,
Reigned in that courtroom silence dread,
And as he ceased, a solemn gloom
Seemed to pervade that crowded room,
And a low, dread muttering ran
Around, from woman, child and man ;
But swifter than a flash of thought,
Down on his desk his hammer brought,
And straight again was silence dread,
O'er all within that courtroom spread ;
Save clocks that ticked upon the wall,
There was no other sound at all ;
You might have heard a feather fall,
So dread did silence all men thrall ;

If there no clocks had ticked, the tomb
Shows no more silence than that room.
And silence kept its dread repose
Till Down from off his seat arose,
And said in low and solemn tone
That thrill'd through marrow, nerve and
    bone,
Stand up, thou prisoner at the bar,
And tell me what thy reasons are,
Why now sentence of death by me
Should not be straight pronounced on
    thee ? "
" I am standing," Ragan replied,
" Is sight unto your eyes denied ?
Your time you need no longer lose,
So just pronounce whate'er you choose ;
Further than these no words I'll say
Ere from your sight I pass away,
And what I speak all men shall see
Is truth, ere yet a month shall flee ;
They'll see as plain as noonday sun,
This crime by me was never done ;
That I am guiltless of the deed
As is the vestal's cross and bead,
O'er which she cons her midnight prayer,
With guarding seraphs watching near.
Suppose I had this murder done,
I would have strove the law to shun ;
And wheresoe'er I cast the dead,
His clothes had also with him sped ;
I ne'er had paused to take away
The robes that did the dead array ;
Down in the pool where he I cast,
His clothes had also with him past ;

And lost within that sable tarn,
I ne'er had ta'en them to my barn,
And hid them there in loft or mow,
As you so warmly told just now;
Why, this to all must plainly show,
I nothing of this murder know.
No, if indeed, this boy be dead,
If by murderer's hands he bled,
Then you, Judge Down, or Hugh Lenore,
Or one that 'gainst me witness bore,
Have done this dread and cruel sin!"
At this Judge Down broke fiercely in:
" It grieves me much to see a wretch
Whose neck the gallows soon shall stretch
For evil deeds that he has done,
And ne'er his fate may hope to shun,
Whom not a law on earth can save,
Nor rescue from a felon's grave,
So grossly lost to every thought
Of remorse for murder he has wrought!
You look as all defiant now,
And gather smiles upon your brow
As though as grand a deed you'd done,
As ever fame for hero won!
So it shall be my duty now,
To show what mercy laws allow
To hinds like you, so fierce and grim,
Who show not, save in form and limb,
That they belong to human kind,
Or God to them a soul consigned.
Now, you, Earl Ragan, hence shall go,
Unto your cell, this court below,
And there in solitude remain
Till this day week shall come again,

And when the week has past away,
For time will swiftly bring the day,
Far quicker than you wish to see,
'Tween the hours of one and three,
You shall be taken from your cell
By the Sheriff, or whom he tell
So to do, and you shall be brought
Upon the gallows, a rope be caught
Around your neck, and you shall hang
Till you are dead! till every pang
And moan, and sign of vital breath
Departs and leaves you grim with death!
May God His wrath on you control,
And have mild mercy on your soul.

V.

This said the Judge with solemn air,
And straight again resumed his chair,
His elbows on his desk he leant,
And o'er his hands his face he bent;
And for a long and dreary space
Thus from the throng he hid his face.
While thus his bulky head he bowed,
There was dead silence 'mongst the crowd,
Save tick of clock, no other sound
Was heard that crowded courtroom round.
With parted lips and staring eyes,
They gazed at him in dumb surprise;
Whether he smiled, or prayed or wept,
While thus concealed his face he kept,
None there could guess who looked on him,
For stirred he neither form nor limb.
Thus his bald crown by them was seen
For twenty minutes, full, I ween.

VI.

From off his hands his face he drew,
And round the courtroom cast his view,
And said, with voice made hoarse with dole,
" Now, I have prayed for this man's soul !
Prayed God would wash away its stain,
And hope I have not asked in vain.
But he's so hardened in his crime,
I fear it is but wasted time
To pray for ruffians such as him,
Whose souls are as a dragon grim.
Repent ! repent ! young man, I say !
Oh, to your God forever pray,
That He may wash your sin away,
And make your spirit bright as day !
For crime let it but feel remorse
Before it treads that unknown course !
Now, Sheriff, take your man away,
I have no other word to say.

VII.

Soon to his gloomy cell below
Did Ragan with the Sheriff go,
And gay he from the courtroom trod,
As though he strolled o'er his own sod—
Amongst his pastures rich and green,
And had his herds around him seen ;
Nor did his stalwart footsteps lag
E'en when he trod the dungeon flag ;
When closed on him the iron door,
And locked was every bolt it bore,
Yea, just as dauntless air he wore,
As he had ever worn before.

VIII.

Soon as the prisoner left their view,
The crowd from out the courtroom drew;
Some left with joy o'er Ragan's doom,
And wished he only filled his tomb—
Fancied him a murderer grim,
As e'er showed human form or limb,
But those who felt this way were few
Compared to all who from there drew—
Some left with heavy grief and dole,
With leaden sorrow in each soul,
For the fate of him they well believed
Ne'er wrought, nor yet the crime con-
    ceived.
Many were there who thought this way,
And such some men were heard to say;
Yet all save two past from that room
Either glad or sad o'er Ragan's doom.
Yes, only two men lingered there
Amidst that courtroom's dusky air.
One was Judge Down, the other man
Was of a build of different plan;
Tall was his form, and broad his breast,
His shoulders mighty strength confess'd,
His thewy limbs were thick and long,
And as the hickory tough and strong;
The fingers of his stalwart hands
Felt less like flesh than iron bands;
His heavy locks of sable hue
Concealed his forehead all from view,
Though it was massive, broad and high,
They hid it from the gazer's eye;
His shaggy eyebrows half concealed
The light his sable orbs revealed;

Enough of them was seen to show
They did intensely flash and glow
With craftiness and subtle wile
As e'er displayed a soul of guile;
His heavy beard revealed no trace
Of any feature in his face,
Nor could you tell if grief or care,
Despair or joy was furrowed there;
His parrot nose of massive frame
Far out from his hairy visage came,
And like an eagle's bill, the end
Did to'rds his hairy mouth descend.
This was the man they called Lenore,
As fierce a fiend as ever wore
The outward form of mortal man.
Since first on earth the race began;
The slyest thief that night or day
To crib or fowlroost bent his way;
False witness 'twas his trade to bear,
And 'gainst the innocent to swear;
Would murder gladly do for meed,
Feel no remorse for foulest deed—
A villain grim from crust to core
As ever trod on dale or moor,
Or ever strode on dungeon floor,
Was this man they called Hugh Lenore.

IX.

Soon as the crowd had past away
And in that room alone were they,
Close to Judge Down strode Hugh Lenore,
And hoarsely said, " Now Judge, the score
Of witnesses that here I brought,
Who how to swear by you were taught,

This evening homeward wend their way,
And ere they leave they wish their pay;
Their orders all have given me
To draw from you their witness fee;
Let's have it straight, my noble Judge,
For all, before they homeward trudge,
Would like their share of ale and grog,
Likewise their fill of wholesome prog,
And buy their winter's stock of food."

X.

Replied the Judge in haughty mood,
As with his small, white, jeweled hand
His golden spectacles he donn'd,
Where eyes beneath intensely blazed,
And on Lenore their gaze he raised.
" Why, you astonish me complete,
Surprise me o'er from head to feet,
In asking such a thing from me,
And now let it the last time be
That I am asked for witness fee,
To pay it I did ne'er agree;
If from me you expected this,
I swear you've reckoned all amiss.
The witnesses you brought to me
I never promised any fee,
Nor gave them hopes of any gear
Although I told them how to swear.
Just what to say in Ragan's case.
So we might murder to him trace,
And him in all this crime detect;
And if they pay for this expect,
Then they will be deceived indeed,
For I've no cash to pay their meed.

Nor do I care one single dime
If here they stay a month of time;
Or if to'rds home they wander hence,
They'll not get drunk at my expense;
And if around this town for spoil
From me, they make the least turmoil,
I'll have them placed in gloomy cell,
And there a month or more they'll dwell.
Where granite flags shall be their bed
Without a straw or rag for spread,
However wild the wintery blast
. Its icy breath around them cast,
Water and meal their drink and bread,
And sometimes be on onions fed."

XI

Thus said the Judge with haughty air,
And backward in his cushioned chair
His bulky head he placed at rest,
Folded his arms across his breast,
One leg athwart the other drew,
A moment down his gaze he threw
Upon his scals of varied hue,
And smiled as if pleased with their view.
While thus he gazed he did not see
The flash of fiendish craft and glee
That in his listener's dark eyes glowed,
Round which black hair abundant flowed.
And made them look like flames that shine
Deep bedded in a sable mine,
Nor saw the visage fierce and grim,
With stalwart form and giant limb,
Which like cloud from volcanoe's brim,
Was fiercely frowning down on him.

And neither spake an ample space,
Though shades of night in rapid race
Were falling in that gloomy place,
And darkening over each man's face.
At length with hoarse and savage tone,
Lenore thus made his feelings known:

XII.

"If what you've said you really mean,
It will be sore for you, I ween;
Judge as you are, o'er all this land,
I dare to 'gainst you lift my hand!
And if from out yon seat you move,
What now I've said I'll swiftly prove
With pistol, or with gleaming knife,
So stir not, if you prize your life!
You shall call in no succor here,
And none shall 'tween us interfere,
Till I have spoken every word
I have to say, and you have heard
The thoughts that labor in my breast,
Which you have thrown in wild unrest.
Though o'er this town you reign and rule
Like tyrant in a village school,
Who plies on all his scourging rod,
Whose pupils tremble at his nod,
Yet me you cannot frighten more
Than rock is scared by waves that roar;
So stir not till you hear me through,
Or I will drive this knife in you!
To say you never promised meed
If we for you would do this deed,
Is firmly now by me denied,
And Judge, I tell you, you have lied!

What call had we to do the deed,
Unless to us you promised meed?
Earl Ragan never injured me,
Nor harmed us in the least degree;
In fact, a kindly heart he bore
To all the wretched, abject poor,
And oft he's eased my hungry mood,
When at his door I've craved for food;
The voice of want he'd ever heed,
And had I not been sore in need,
I ne'er on him had sworn this deed,
For less than thrice your promised meed.
And there is Musgrave! that poor boy,
His father's only heir and joy!
Think you his life had been destroyed
If you for meed had not employed
The hand that basely shed his blood,
And cast him in the whirlpool's flood?
Now, by his death, you will fall heir
To all he owned the largest share;
And by Earl Ragan's fall, your kin
A fair and wealthy bride will win;
And this had never chanced, if we
By crimes all of the first degree,
Had not set both your pathways free;
So pay the promised meed to me.
If this to us you don't bestow,
The truth to all the land I'll show."

                    XIII.

As thus he spake, the night apace,
Had so filled all that courtroom's space,
The speaker scarcely there could trace
The features of his listener's face;

And saw not either frown or smile,
If any gathered there the while;
But plain his eyes, Lenore could see,
From these mute rage was flashing free;
And as on him they often turned,
Sheen through the gloom their fire burn'd
Like flashing sparks at night we greet,
When steel and flint abruptly meet;
So in his eyes the mingled tide
Of chasing rage and hate was spied;
And brightly did they flash through gloom
That gathered in that dreary room.
Scarce on his lips Hugh's voice had died,
Than thus to him the Judge replied:

XIV.

" Think not, vain fool, by any threat,
That you can force from me a debt,
Even if such I owed to you,
And it had long been overdue;
I tell you I've no cash at all,
To give at any ruffian's call!
You talk of things you've done for me.
Now, what are they all? come let's see
The mighty wonders you have done:
You've slain for me my sister's son.
George Musgrave, a frail, worthless boy,
Whose living did my peace annoy;
And by his death, 'tis true, I heir
A broad estate of pastures rare;
I wrote the will she left behind,
And framed it just to suit my mind;
At her child's death, I made it so
Most all her wealth to me would go;

And to her husband, Richard, gave
Just what of hers I did not crave,
A little house upon the hill,
With grounds enough for him to till,
Where he might earn his daily bread,
If not too lazy life he led.
But not one foot of all her land,
You see, is yet at my command ;
The will distinctly says, a year
Must pass from the death of this heir
Before I shall lay any claim
To lands she left in my own name;
Through this time Richard is the lord
Of her dominions fair and broad.
So since a year must pass away
Before they come beneath my sway,
I'll have to wait through all this time
Ere I from them shall win a dime.
I cannot pay you for your deed,
But when I can, will give the meed ;
So take not my delay so ill,
You were a witness to her will ;
Yes, you were present when 'twas made,
And was for all your trouble paid ;
You know just how that will doth read,
So do not ask me now for meed.
And as concerns my other kin,
Why, he has yet his bride to win,
But when in this he doth succeed,
I'll pay you nobly for your deed ;
But you a little while must wait,
Till he gets hold of her estate ;
Then jolly times he'll give the boys,
Who helped him to obtain his toys.

You boast that you the truth will show,
On me the stain of murder throw,
Why people round would only think
That you were overfraught with drink :
And all that heard you, far and wide,
Would firmly think you only lied ;
I stand too high for such as you
To soil me, though your tales were true ;
The less you talk about your crime,
Now, or at any other time,
You'll find is better for your weal,
Or you the hangman's rope may feel ;
My bank account is very low,
Far smaller than I like to show,
And not a dime to-night I spare
To you or any with you here ;
If you and them are sore in need,
Why, you and them this night can speed
Unto some rich man's mansion here
And rob him of his shining gear ;
Many a house this town can show
Round us within a pebble's throw,
Where bureau drawers and chests do hold
Huge piles of silver and of gold ;
Go, all of you, and take your share,
If not afraid the task to dare.
Should any of your men be caught,
And to this court for trial brought,
Though it be proven clear as light
That it was them who robbed that night,
Trust me to fix the jury so
They'll let the guilty guiltless go.
There, now, I have no more to say,
So please to go from me away."

XV.

" I'll go from you," the other said,
" But ere from you my footsteps tread,
Say, give to me some little gold,
For all of us are dry and cold ;
They also need a little food,
'Twill make them all of better mood ;
I'll take whatever you'll allow,
And straight divide it 'mongst them now."
" I told you thrice distinct and clear,
To-night I can you nothing spare."
" You mean to say your bureaus hold
No coin of silver nor of gold ? "
" I do." " Then we must find a way
Wherein to earn more ready pay."
" I hope you will; I cannot give
A dime to-night, true as you live."
" Perhaps to-morrow ? " " No, not then.
At all." Well, Judge, just tell me when ? "
" Let's see. 'Twill be one full half year.
Ere I have any cash to spare."
" All right, Judge ; but I trust my men
For pay will scarcely ask you then ;
Perhaps you'll never pay the meed
For which they stand so sore in need.
Now farewell, Judge, but ere I go,
One little thing I'd have you know ;
Perhaps George Musgrave is not dead,
But yet is living ! "

XVI.

With heavy tread
Lenore from out that courtroom strode,
And past along a narrow road.

The rain was pouring hard and fast,
And in dense gloom were all things cast,
Yet swift through mud and rain he strode,
Until he reached a lone abode;
Right soon the door he open threw,
And in the lofty dwelling drew.
There seated round, a motley crew,
All waiting him, there met his view.
There were gathered men from every clime
Known to summer's smile or winter's rime,
From every nation 'neath the sun,
Where breezes blow or waters run.
And these were those Lenore had brought,
And what to say the Judge had taught,
So they would know just how to swear,
And witness 'gainst Earl Ragan bear.
Many a tall and brawny form,
As ever moved in shine or storm,
As ever trod through valleys green,
Among that motley crew were seen:
There some with forms and features plann'd
In comely mould, were 'mongst them
    scann'd,
Mortals, whom, to behold their mien,
If in some other sphere 'twere seen,
Save in a den of loathsome crime,
Where only outlaws pass'd their time,
No one had thought who had them seen.
They trod a path of life so mean;
That they were villains low and vile,
With spirits steeped in fraud and wile;
Yet some of these were full of wit,
And knew just how to handle it,
Had language of a fluent flow,
Could much of solid learning show;

Could sentences together fit,
As well as ever scholar writ;
Some well were versed in every art,
And all the poets knew by heart;
Could sing a song or tell a tale,
As well as quaff their grog and ale.
Histories of all lands they knew,
The ancient and the modern too,
And oft some points from these they drew,
When on such things their fancies flew ;
They gave the dates of battles fought,
As true as ever teacher taught.
Knew all the heroes names that led,
Also which triumphed and which fled,
Or which in battle harness bled ;
Knew all the numbers of the dead ;
Knew all the styles of arms displayed,
And numbers on each side arrayed ;
Right well all hymns and psalms they
        knew,
And sung them to their music, too ;
Knew holy writ from end to end,
Had all by rote the prophets penn'd,
Knew everything these prophets wrought,
Knew every sacred truth they taught,
With which their holy souls were fraught.
Such were these men who here were
        brought
Together on grim Ruin's brink,
Through love of alcoholic drink ;
Through laziness, through love of sloth,
To the embraces nothing loth,
Of passions vilest and most low,
Which cause mind and body's overthrow ;

Which twine around the yielding soul
And bind it fast in their control,
Around it build their iron wall, ·
Hard, massive, solid, thick and tall,
With iron floor and roof it all,
Until they cannot burst their thrall,
Nor from their cursed fetters crawl
Although a universe should fall !
Lost wretches, who, in forms of men,
Together herd in loathsome den,
To plot out crimes the most obscene,
And of the most ferocious mien
That mournful nature yet could show
Midst all her misery and woe.

XVII.

A spacious stove they sat around,
The kind which are in taverns found,
Which well the room with comfort
      crown'd ;
And in one corner stood the bar,
Arrayed with bottle, jug and jar,
With pitcher, glasses, and canteen,
As always are in barrooms seen
When they are kept in order good.
Behind this bar the landlord stood,
A man of short but portly frame,
And Blockly Wallace, styled by name.
A happy, jolly soul was he,
Forever full of jest and glee,
Who took his treats right often free,
Whene'er the cash for them he'd see ;
And ne'er his features wore a frown,
Save when some thirsty, burly clown,

Such as are found in every town,
Would call for drinks and drain them down,
Then wipe his lips and pass away,
Saying he would pay some other day !
Then angry frowns his brow o'ercast,
While from his lips grim curses past.
But long as he could sell his trash
And for it get the ready cash,
A jolly, happy soul was he,
As traveler in the land might see.

XVIII.

A brute in form, a brute in mind,
To every sense of virtue blind,
A wily and a tricky knave,
To all the lowest lusts a slave ;
Depraved of heart, and base of soul,
Where vilest passions hold control,
That all the realm of nature knows,
Just such as mostly are all those
Who make their living in this way,
No matter where we them survey.
Go search the nations wide and far,
The landlord of a whiskey bar
Is one of those most vile and low
The family of man can show.
If this is not true of all those men,
'Tis of the landlord of this den ;
The vilest drink the world could show
'Mongst grog holes most obscure and low,
With smiling face he freely sold,
To men or women, young or old ;
Without it they ne'er went away,
If they but had the cash to pay ;

And when o'ercome with flaming drink,
They drunk upon the floor would sink,
And lie as senseless as the dead,
If all their cash was spent and fled
He'd drag them o'er his beastly floor,
And roughly spurn them from his door,
Leave the all helpless, senseless form,
Unsheltered midst the fiercest storm.
And often on a winter's morn
Has some poor abject wretch forlorn,
Half hid amongst the snow been found,
Stark dead and frozen to the ground.
And lying right beside the door,
Whose threshold he had spurn'd them o'er.
And when the frozen corpse was found,
Its weeping orphans flocked around,
And widow with her sad pale face,
Where woe had left its lasting trace,
The fountains of whose eyes had dried,
No more there balm to grief supplied;
Poor wretch, whose unutterable dole,
Had settled tearless on her soul;
Whose midnight watchings and whose
    tears,
Had lasted and had flowed for years;
But now they both had ceased for one
That she had loved and doted on,
Whom she in early youth had wed,
With whom a happy life had led,
In home devoid of every strife,
With pleasures scattered round her rife;
Happier pair earth could not show,
Than were those twain long years ago,
Ere he began to pass his time
Within that loathsome den of crime.

And there by drink made wild of mood,
His wealth spent for that landlord's good,
What should have only gone for food
For his sad wife and starving brood.
Yes, ere the landlord of that inn
Won all his heart through grog and gin,
From his fond wife and children all
And lured him to untimely fall,
Solely to win the cash he brought,
For this, naught else that landlord sought;
He knew his nature weak and frail,
As chaff that scatters on the gale,
Was easy led by such as he,
And made to spend his earnings free,
Till he was but a beggar poor,
Fit subject for an almshouse floor;
Then kindly welcomed him no more,
To joys within that landlord's door.

XIX.

What would that heartless landlord say,
When midst the snow the dead man lay?
When in the early morn was found,
The stiffened corpse froze to the ground?
While o'er it orphans shed the tear,
And all the widows sighs could hear?
Did he pour comfort in their ear,
Or soothe their sorrow, wild and drear?
" Come, take that man from hence, I say,
I will not have him in my way;
Nor will I have one moment more
This weeping howl about my door;
You make your noise too cursed loud,
You'll be gathering here a crowd,

Nor do I wish the town to see
A loafer of so low degree
Lying thus early at my door.
He's not dead, he's drunk; nothing more!
I wish such good-for-nothing trash
Would stay just where they spend their
    cash!
He's long been getting drunk elswhere,
Then coming to annoy me here;
A full round month has passed, I trow,
Since last I saw him until now;
And then I told him plain as day,
To from my tavern keep away;
That he must give his drinking o'er,
Not keep his home so wretched poor.
To get as drunk as he is now,
Last night he must have been, I trow,
Where grog was freely given him,
To buy, his cash was all too slim."
Thus, oft has he been heard to say,
When such a scene before him lay.

XX.

A happy smile his features wore,
When in his place came Hugh Lenore,
For scores of drinks he knew he'd sell,
And get the ready cash as well;
It made his heart with rapture leap,
To think what shining spoil he'd reap
Soon as Lenore paid all his men
Their fees, for which they waited then;
Right well he knew that every mite
Would come to him for drink that night.
It made his soul with rapture boil
To think upon his coming spoil;

So heartily he hailed Lenore
Soon as he trod his bar before.
" Welcome," he said, " my dear old boy ! "
And grasped his hand with seeming joy.
" Come take a right good drink with me,
For you I am real glad to see !
And for your sake, your men I'll call
Unto the bar and treat them all.
So come up, all you boys ! "　At the word
From out his seat each ruffian stirr'd,
Past swift across the sanded floor
And stood the spacious bar before ;
Where shone beneath a glowing light
Long lines of tumblers shining bright ;
Where huge decanters also glowed,
And ruddy grog within them showed.

XXI.

Each filled his glass unto the brim—
Some till the juice o'erflowed the rim,
And glad their eyes were seen to blink,
As they raised up the ruddy drink,
To lips and mouth that craved it sore
As ever such have craved before.
Down went the juice of ruddy glow
Into each maw with rapid flow,
Like streams the mountains sometimes
　　show,
That sudden fall in gurge below,
That pass away with gurgling roar
And never meet the eyesight more.
Scarce was the treat of Wallace o'er
Than drinks were called by Hugh Lenore ;
Again each glass was filled, again
Did each his glass of liquor drain ;

But ere had past one minute o'er,
" Fill up again ! " cried Hugh Lenore,
" For better juice was ne'er distill'd ! "
Right soon again were glasses filled
With juice that 'neath the lamplight
    glow'd,
And swift to craving maws it flow'd.
Soon as 'twas drank, cried Hugh Lenore,
" Now, Wallace, when my men want more,
As water, let them have it free,
And you can charge it all to me ;
Trust them, you need not be afraid ;
At morning I will see you paid."
" All right ! " the other answer made,
As he with smiles Lenore surveyed.

XXII.

Scarcely these words had breathed Le-
    nore,
Than o'er the threshold of the door
Came old Judge Down with hasty stride,
And with the Sheriff at his side :
" Drinks for the house ! " the Sheriff said,
As to the bar the Judge he led.
" Come Wallace, let us have the best
Your house can show to cherished guest !
For Down and I with you will stay,
Till morning drives the night away,
And 'tween to-morrow's dawn and now,
High mirth we'll have if you'll allow ;
The Judge's wife has gone from town,
And save but one old toothless clown,
No other living soul, I ween,
Is in his stately mansion seen ;

Nor do I think it wise nor right
For the Judge to be alone at night,
So I have brought him here with me
To drink and have a little glee.
So deal us out your choicest wine,
And let us feel its glow divine ;
This night is dark o'er moor and hill,
We'll drive away its damp and chill ;
Let tempests howl just as they will,
With joy our hearts to-night shall thrill.
Earth drinks the rain, the stream and rill,
Yet she is ever thirsty still ;
So why should Nature take it ill
If mortal also drinks his fill ?
Bless him who fashioned first the mill,
And taught how whiskey to distill !
Or rum or gin or any drink
Which makes us joyous feel and think.
Come, Wallace, deal your grog around,
To all within this barroom found ;
For no one in this place to-night
Shall sigh for drink till morning's light !
And no man amongst us all,
Though he should stagger to the wall,
And prone upon the floor should fall,
Too dead to either move or crawl,
Shall be considered downright drunk,
Unles his drinks by him be slunk,
No matter if he cannot tell
The difference 'tween a harp and bell,
Or east from west or north from south,
So he lifts drinks up to his mouth,
And pours them down his gullet right,
He shan't be deem'd real drunk to-night !

So let the tempest rage without,
We within will sing and shout!
Let whirlwinds make their wailing noise,
As if they moaned o'er buried joys,
But we shall laugh and shout sing,
And make with mirth this barroom ring;
We far away all care shall fling,
For joy shall o'er us flap her wing!
Fill up, again, my jolly boys,
'Twill make your spirits thrill with joys;
There's untold bliss within the cup
When with good drink we've filled it up,
It, need no mortal fear to sup,
Nor lips right widely for it dup,
Whoever does is a worthless nup,
Or is Dame Nature's common pup!
And void of brains as iron tup.

XXIII.

O'er moor and hill the tempests bray
And tear the limbs of trees away,
Dark, inky clouds the skies o'ercast,
And rain and sleet is falling fast;
The shutters slam, the windows jar,
And doors screak loud 'gainst bolt and
 bar,
The watchdog in his kennel sleeps,
Not any watch to-night he keeps,
If any sound to-night he hears
He scarce to it will prick his ears,
For he will deem it is the sound
Of tempests rending trees around,
Or falling sheds to atoms hurl'd
By storms that keep awake the world;

Just hark, now, how they moan and roar,
And rain hard 'gainst yon window pour!
A better night I never saw
For men who do not care for law,
To search a rich man's bureau draw
Or make in locks and bolts a flaw,
So they can open wide the chest
Where hidden diamonds snugly rest
And for its gold and silver quest
In just the way it suits them best.
Were I a thief, I would not miss
A night for reaping spoil like this,
I would be working, hand and brain,
To see what rich men's homes contain ;
And I should take an ample share
Of all I found of shining gear,
I'd not be poor another day
If I found gold to take away !
Come, fill up, boys, another dram,
Nor care how storms the shutters slam,
Nor how the doors on hinges jar
And thump against both bolt and bar,
Nor how the raindrops pelt and dash
On any rich man's window sash ;
Nor will we care for hoards that rest
In any secret drawer or chest,
For them to-night we shall not quest,
We love this barroom's comforts best.
So drain your cups my jolly boys,
For grog contains earth's chiefest joys ! "

XXIV.

While thus his mirth the Sheriff showed,
From jugs to cups the liquor flowed,

From these to yearning mouths it past,
And into craving maws was cast,
Till all who stood that bar before
Had taken twelve huge drinks, and more ;
Then straight to a huge arm-chair
That stood beside a table there,
The Judge with reeling body drew,
His arms upon the table threw,
On these his head he swiftly bowed,
And was the first of all the crowd
Who from his share of drinking shrunk,
Or seem'd the least way sleepy drunk.
Thus, while was heard his heavy snore,
The Sheriff whispered to Lenore,
" Say, is your brain as lump of flint,
That even steel on it can print
Not e'en the slightest mark nor dint ?
That you to-night can take no hint ?
Have I not told you, plain as day,
Down's wife and servants are away,
And not a soul to-night doth sleep
Or watch within his mansion keep ?
E'en his old hostler is not there,
For just before we started here
I saw that he was sent elsewhere ;
He can't return ere break of day,
Though he should gallop all his way.
I know some of his closets hold
Huge bags of silver and of gold,
So why not send some of your men
To overhawl at once his den,
And bring out everything they can ?
No harm to steal from such a man !
So send them now."

XXV.

"Did you not see,
Ere we of drinks had taken three,
Five men from out this tavern go?
Why, it's been two hours or so.
Perhaps your mind was too intent
On drinks, to notice when they went.
They've gone to do this very thing,
And shortly here his gold they'll bring;
His silver ware, or any kind
Of spoil they in his house can find;
And well I know if such they see,
They'll help themselves most amply free!"

XXVI

"Well done!   I hope they will it find,
And leave not there a mite behind;
For slyer, meaner thief than him
Was never jailed in dugeon grim!
When you and him this eve, Lenore,
In the court talked your secrets o'er,
I and my daughter plainly heard
The speech of both, yes, every word.
What pass'd at first we did not hear,
For then we were not quite so near;
But when the place grew dark with gloom
We crept within a little room,
Where all destinctly we could hear
Each syllable you uttered there,
That he refused to pay your meed,
That you declared you did the deed
For which Earl Ragan just was tried.
I guess by you is not denied?

For we heard it all, and at last,
Just ere from out the room you past,
We heard you say, you can't forget,
George was not dead, but living yet!
Now, say, Lenore, be frank and free,
Nor hide a secret now from me;
You know long years I've been your friend,
And one will prove whate'er your end,
And scarcely need I tell you such,
Since I have done for you so much;
That Down will pay no slightest meed
To you nor yours for any deed,
You know is true as here we stand,
So don't with murder stain your hand,
Nor damn your soul through endless time
By helping him in any crime!
If you can prove that Ragan's free
Of murder, though he guilty be,
Far larger meed for it you'll see
Than Down to you will ever give,
Although a thousand years you live!
Now, tell me truth, say is it so
That some one murdered Musgrave?"
       " No!"
But ask me now not any more,
Just give this cursed subject o'er
For all the balance of to-night,
To-morrow I will set you right.
But cannot, and I will not now,
Till fitter time and place allow.
Come, call up drinks again!" "I will,
For I, myself, feel dry and chill:
Come, Wallace, deal the liquor round,
To all within this barroom found.

Although the Judge, I really think,
Is all too drunk his share to drink.
Give me his share of liquor now,
And I will pour it o'er his brow!
He can't now drink its ruddy wave,
With it his classic head I'll lave!
I care not though it roil him sore,
It o'er his crown I now will pour!"

XXVII.

As this he said to'rds Down he drew,
And o'er his head the liquor threw!
But so dead drunk was the old knave,
He did not feel the chilly wave.
And though it flowed o'er brow and face,
He stirr'd not from his resting place;
One heavy snore was all he gave,
As o'er him flowed the icy wave.
But from the treat none other shrank,
Each gladly there his whiskey drank.
And scarcely was the drinking o'er,
Than open flew the barroom door;
Scarce was it ope'd than through it came,
Five men of tall and burly frame,
Though one with age was gray and bent;
They were the men Lenore had sent
Away more than three hours before,
To thoroughly Down's house explore;
To search from cellar unto roof,
And from no closet keep aloof;
To open every door and chest,
To all around for treasure quest;
And not to leave a thing behind
For which they any use might find;

When they possessed of all became.
To then straight set the house in flame ;
To kindle flames within it so
It unto ruin sure would go,
And on the earth be swiftly spread,
In one huge pile of embers red,
Before the eye of any man
The fast destroying blaze should scan.

XXVIII.

Soon to the eyes of Hugh Lenore
Those men displayed the spoil they bore ;
Huge sacks of coin they with them brought,
And silver-ware most costly wrought ;
Jewels set thick with starry gems.
Which clusterd dense as grapes on stems :
And many things of price untold,
Like mugs, wrought out of solid gold.

XXIX.

Three sacks of coin they gave Lenore,
He one of these to Wallace bore,
Saying, as to that man he drew,
While to his hand the sack he threw,
"Take out of this all that we owe,
And in your till the balance throw,
For in my mind there is no doubt,
We long ere morn shall drink it out."
When this he said, to'rds Down he sped,
And right above his classic head,
The other bags he fiercely shook,
And sad, "You sly old rascal, look !
This eve he falsely swore to me
That not a mite of cash had he

To pay us the promised meed,
Though we for it were sore in need;
But little dreams he, now, I ween,
That we have swept his coffers clean!
It serves him right, for thief more mean,
Dame Nature's eyes have never seen.
Come, Wallace, round the liquor hand,
My throat is dry as desert sand,
That is by burning tempests fann'd,
Like that found in Sahara's land!"
" Yea, pass it round!" the Sheriff cried,
My throat and lips are also dried,
As is the leaf in autumn's bower,
Where falls no dew, no frost, nor shower;
Yes, dry as is the fleshless bone,
That in the scorching flame is thrown!
Come let's drain our glasses now,
To yon old Judge with classic brow,
The slyest knave in form of man
That ever lived since earth began—
Amongst us all he's lost his sway,
And waxes weaker day by day,
But may his shadow ne'er grow less,
Till him in prison garb we dress!
When that time comes, I will not fail,
If still I'm keeper of the jail,
To give him just such wholesome fare
As I to any friend can spare;
Just such pure food to him I'll give,
He will, indeed, most jolly live.
Right oft he did of me request,
That I would feed some prison guest
For whom he had conceived foul hate,
On hashes mix'd with powder'd slate,

Or mush stirred up with dust and sand,
Or any gritty filth at hand.
But him I'll fodder all the while
In a most luxuriant style;
I'll give him turnips boiled with chives,
And best of honey from my hives;
No grog nor ale shall wet his food,
Nor satisfy his thirsty mood,
Though he may beg me o'er and o'er!

XXX.

As thus he spake, a mighty roar,
Like billows toss'd on hollow shore
When tempests ocean's depths explore,
Distinct within their ears was cast
Above the roar of midnight blast;
And from the bar in haste they sped,
To see whence came that tumult dread.
All, all the cloudy skies o'erhead
Were crimsoned to a ruddy red;
For some huge building far away,
Did one vast blaze of flame display!
Its roof and walls were falling down
And sending sparks all o'er the town.
More broad and higher shot the flame,
And redder still the skies became.
Swift to the Judge sped Hugh Lenore,
And from the room his form he bore :
" See yonder, Judge!" he hoarsely cried,
" Was ever grander scene espied ?
Your house is all ablaze!"   But he
No answer made, and seemed to be
All too dead drunk to hear or see.

PART IV.

I.

All things within wide Nature's round
Are wrapped in mystery profound
To him who has no utter clue
To pierce the subtle secrets through ;
Amidst a labyrinth strange he moves,
Which more and more intricate proves
As he its mazes strives to thread
With weary feet and aching head,
Till suddenly a stream of light
Dispels his being's sable night,
And straight he gains the mystic clue,
And threads those mazes through and
    through,
Till there's no fear he'll lose his way
Where'er he shall that labyrinth stray ;
For not a spot within its range
To him is either new or strange.
All mysteries in nature wrought
Are with hope and fear alternate fraught,
And every one is overspread
With strange, bewitching awe and dread ;
For when we all its mazes thread,
Ah ! whither will we then be led ?
When we it to an issue bring,
Will we find joy or sorrowing ?
Where will it end ?   Ah, answer where !
And is it woe or pleasure there ?

II.

God made all mysteries there be,
And greatest one of all is He;
We grapple with this mystery
As though we strove to stop the sea
From its eternal rise and fall,
And fetter it in human thrall;
Or strove our puny arms to cast
Around the Andes structure vast!
Or, just as fruitless, strove to place
Their shadows in a babe's embrace!
As easy for the human hand
To count one by one the grains of sand
Found all throughout vast Nature's clime
Within a moment's space of time,
As thread His mysteries sublime!
Yet, what a pleasing sense of awe
And dread they round the spirit draw,
When mongst his mysteries so strange,
In contemplative mood we range.
Why are the mountains made so high,
With summits frowning at the sky,
As if they were to all estranged?
Why so stupendously arranged?
Why have small grains together grown
To such enormous heights of stone?
And though but barrenness they show,
With peak cloud-capped and robed in
     snow,
Yet, mysteries around them roll
That please the eye and charm the soul!

How fascinating to behold
Their lofty crags so hoar and old!
How grand to view their giant forms,
Though showing wreck of time and storms.
As peak on peak they proudly rise,
As if to prop the azure skies!
How long has stood this mountain land?
And how much longer will it stand?
Are thoughts which make the mind re-
  volve,
But which poor man will never solve;
And for this truth the heights control
Mysteries pleasing to his soul.
Turning from what the mountains show
To contemplate the plains below,
Why are they lasting as the hills,
Whose adamantine summit fills
The whole wide tract of plains below,
With shadows from its head of snow,
As if on them it proudly frown'd?
Why are plains such level ground?
Why there no rocky mountains seen?
And then, why is their grass so green?
Is it because it is a hue
That's pleasing for the eye to view?
Then why does greenness charm the eye?
Azure charms it when it looks on high!
And wherefore does the damp, cold earth
To such lovely flowers give birth?
Wherefore so fragrant is the rose?
Why do such charms in it repose?
Why is the violet so sweet,
With span of life so brief and fleet?
And why the lily of the vale
Formed all so delicate and frail?

Why daisies form'd in such a plan ?
These all are mysteries to man !
As are all things in nature broad,
Which only He shall solve, whose sword
Shall cut the Gordian knot in twain,
Which binds together Nature's reign.

III.

Why are the oceans made so vast,
Such depths of waters in them cast ?
The mind will question of the soul,
When the eye sees the billows roll ;
And tossing high their awful forms,
Roused by chariots of the storms ;
Or sees them resting calm and mild,
Like some slumbering new-born child
Sleeping beneath the noonday's shine,
With features wrapped in smiles divine,
Are secrets He alone can solve,
Who them with rage and storms involve !
And why do on their cycles march
Such myriad stars through heaven's arch ?
Why do they shine so glowing bright ?
Is it to gladden this world's night ?
Are they, too, peopled, like this place,
With some frail, shortlived, mortal race,
Whose grandest pleasures end in woe,
And scarcely e'er is free from throe ?
Or is their race of different plan,
And more supremely blest than man ?
Without a thought of care or woe,
And all unknown to every throe ?
Unknown to storm, or time or change,
But midst eternal pleasures range ?

Or can the sun midst all his glow
Too any race of beings show?
If so, then is their nature, plan,
Like those on earth His glories scan?
Or are they forms of grander mould
Than earthly things shall e'er behold?
Beings with natures all sublime,
As is his own effulgent clime?
Or dwelleth on the moon's sad face,
A mortal or immortal race?
And are they, like her mournful glow,
A mixture all of fear and woe?
When did those myriad worlds in space
First take amidst the void their place,
'Neath order, harmony's control,
First on their destined cycles roll?
And how much longer will they move;
To those laws obedient prove?
Will they forever live and shine,
And shed on earth their light divine?
Will all their fabric and their plan
Dissolve in death like mortal man,
And never more be seen? These! these!
Are fascinating mysteries!
Filling the soul with awe and fear,
As though it felt its Maker near!
Mysteries with wonder rife,
Profound and dread as death and life!
Yet, no more mystery is death,
Than is the mystery of breath!
And none these mysteries shall solve,
Save Him who made those worlds revolve;
Who with His hand created breath,
As well as fashioned grisly death.

IV.

Such thoughts as these fill'd Ragan's soul,
Thrall'd it 'neath their sublime control ;
Yea, forced it all beneath their sway,
The evening of that gloomy day.
They'd convicted him of murder grim,
And had in dungeon fettered him,
And doomed him to a death of shame
Upon the gallows' ghastly frame.
On prison walls his gaze he turn'd,
With eye and brain that throbbed and
    burn'd ;
All things around were wrapp'd in night,
Black as e'er met the vision's sight.
So was one mystery his soul
Could not in any way unroll ;
'Twas tangled all too much for him
To pierce its fabric dark and grim
In any way at all ; the more
He strove its mazes to explore,
Yet still the darker and more drear
Did its strange labyrinth appear.
Why they on him had cast the stain
Of murder, he could not explain ;
This was a mystery, to him
All unexplorable and grim !
One all so wrapp'd in night profound,
He could no part of it expound ;
To him 'twas strange, a mystery,
He did in all wide nature see.

V.

Why, why Bolton and Hugh Lenore,
On him the crime of murder swore,

He could not tell, he could not see,
To him 'twas strangest mystery!
For ne'er by deed nor word nor thought
To them an unkind act he'd wrought.
In fact, whene'er they came his way,
And sore in need and faint were they,
He freely gave them drink and food
And satisfied their hungry mood;
Ne'er aloof from them he stood,
But wrought them kindliness and good.
Why they should strive to work his fall.
He could not tell nor see at all.
And also, why that drove of men,
Whom he had never seen till then,
Should have so falsely sworn 'gainst him,
And charged him with a crime so grim,
He could not see, he could not tell,
All in dark mystery did dwell!
And while amidst his dungeon's gloom
He pondered o'er his coming doom,
While thick and heavy came his breath,
O'er thoughts of meeting felon's death,
A light he saw, a step he heard,
Which just outside his dungeon stirr'd:
He heard each lock and bolt and bar,
Thrown back in haste with sullen jar,
And the huge, solid iron door,
Which was with rust thick coated o'er,
And was on creaking hinges hung.
Was swift but gently open swung;
And o'er the threshold lightly came
A maid of tall and comely frame—
A maiden glorious of mien,
As ever trod in court of queen—

As ever trod on rock or green—
As e'er mongst womankind was seen—
As ever smiled with beaming brow,
Through all the ages until now!
Yea, she was beautiful and fair,
With rosy cheeks and wavy hair;
With ruby lips and pearly teeth,
And bosom fair as frost on heath;
With eyes blue as the realm above,
Yet, full of pity, light and love;
With swan-like neck, round, snowy arms,
As ever graced the queen of charms;
With plump, soft hands as white as snow,
Where did no signs of jewels glow;
And though no gems were on them shown,
Yet if the fairest queen could own
A hand so plump and soft and fair,
No gems nor rings were needed there.

VI.

The Sheriff's daughter, was that maid,
And she, the only help and aid
He kept within that prison wall,
To help him in his daily call;
And when her sire was away
She o'er that prison held full sway.
With lantern in her hand she came,
Which round her poured a ruddy flame,
And swift dispell'd the sable gloom
Which until then had fill'd that room.
" Ragan," she said, " I'll set you free,
For sounds have whispered unto me
That you, as my own self, am clear
Of charges that have placed you here!

And this is true, I know you'll prove—
All stain from off your name remove;
So fly you hence with all your haste.
If you prize your life no moment waste!
My father's horse is strong and swift.
You take him as my parting gift;
He is saddled, and doth remain
Tied to a tree in yonder lane;
Bound to the harness you will find
A garb all of the peasant's kind,
So do yourself in it array,
And cast this prison garb away.
Judge Down, Lenore, and all those men
Whose oathes have doom'd you to this den,
And to a death most grim and dread.
Have to the inn of Wallace sped;
High mirth they hold o'er wine, I trow.
And they perhaps are drunk ere now;
My father keeps them there to-night,
To more securely make your flight;
And there, I ween, till morn they'll stay,
So, Ragan, go not by that way,
Lest they should chance to stop your flight,
And bring you back ere morning's light.
For grim, indeed, your fate would be,
If these fierce fiends your flight should see.
But inky gloom doth all o'ercast,
And fiercely sweeps the wintry blast,
Hard fall the driving rain and sleet,
I trow no one to-night you'll meet.
Go, Ragan, go, no longer stay,
And may God guide you on your way!
Oh! may His kind, protecting arm
Shield my poor Ragan from all harm!

I call you mine, and when away,
O'er land or sea from me you stray.
Know this, there is one soul on earth,
Who wishes you naught else but mirth!
Yes, Ragan, one who loves you so,
She o'er the world with you would go;
Where waters run or breezes blow,
And share your peril, pain or woe!
Yes, when from her you're far away,
Oh, sometimes think on Ellen Fay,
Who'll think of you both night and day!
Now fly, I have naught else to say!"

VII.

The steed he found, his garb he changed,
And fast he o'er the country ranged,
League after league he sped that night,
Was far away ere morning's light;
On, on he sped through sleet and hail,
And through a cold December gale;
O'er twenty miles he rode that night,
Nor man nor woman met his sight;
Through storm and darkness still he rode
Until he reached a lone abode,
That in a swampy thicket stood,
Built out of mud and bark and wood;
A dismal and as lone a bield
As e'er from storm did mortal shield.
Through his past life, three times or more,
He'd cross'd its gloomy threshold o'er
And trod upon that shanty's floor,
Met there its inmate, Hugh Lenore.
He gazed upon that grim abode
Through seams the logs and mud wall
    showed;

Within he saw a taper glowed,
He tied his steed and to'rds it strode ;
He moved to where its strong oak door
Stood jarring to the tempest's roar ;
Long paused he ere he touched the latch,
To see what sound his ear might catch ;
But not a sound therein he heard,
Naught, naught within that shanty stirr'd ;
If any noise there was within,
'Twas smothered by the tempest's din ;
For hail and sleet with steady pour,
Down hard upon that shanty bore ;
And tempests howling mongst the trees,
Made round a noise like stormy seas,
When them on shores the storm-king
 drives,
And with rock and blast each billow
 strives.
Long stood he midst the tempest's roar,
Was just about to strike the door,
And call the wife of Hugh Lenore,
As sudden noise he heard within,
Which rose above the tempest's din ;
He heard a threat, a curse and blow,
Something seem'd on the floor to go,
In heavy, headlong overthrow ;
With it he heard a stifled groan,
As though some wretch were knocked or
 thrown.
Then came a silence long and dread,
Though all within that hut were dead.

IX.

He paused awhile, then on the door
He struck, and called for Hugh Lenore ;

Scarce had he made his presence known,
Than some one to the door had flown :
" Who's there ? " a woman's voice swift
    cried :
" A stranger ! " Ragan straight raplied.
" Amidst these swamps I've lost my way ;
Beneath your shelter let me stay
Out of this storm till break of day,
And you I will most amply pay."
Whether 'twas insatiate greed
To get from him the promised meed,
For the few short hours he craved
Of shelter from the storm that raved,
Or whether she thought the while,
To let him in with friendly style,
Bid him kind welcome from the storm,
And while he stretched his weary form
Beside her hearth in slumber deep,
She might to him with dagger creep,
And shed his life, then seize all gold
She might amongst his clothes behold,
I cannot rightly tell you now,
But 'twas for cause like this I trow,
That she unbarr'd and ope'd the door
And bade him pass the threshold o'er,
And shelter find from storms that roar'd,
And pelting hail and sleet that pour'd

X.

Across the threshold swift he past,
And round the hut his vision cast ;
Upon the floor George Musgrave lay,
With visage pale as snow-white clay,
And gazed on him with mute dismay.

There on the wall of that abode
A brace of loaded pistols glowed,
These, swift within his hand he caught,
And to the wall his back he brought,
And did confront with savage air
That trembling and astonished pair,
Who all bewilderd on him stared.
So was his face o'ergrown with beard—
So robed was he with sleet and hail.
Which glowed o'er him like silver mail,
And made him look so tall and grim—
So huge of shoulders and of limb,
George Musgrave recognized not him
Nor did the wife of Hugh Lenore
Then know the man she stood before.
Though lay but one brief year between
The time she last that man had seen.
Each seem'd afraid to frown or smile,
And silent gazed at him the while.

XI.

At length he gave a heavy groan,
And said in low sepulchral tone,
"This night to God for aid I cried,
Nor was His help to me denied,
But one short while I had to wait,
Ere came the day to meet my fate.
And though no utter chance I saw,
For me to 'scape the cruel law,
Yet faith in God was rooted fast,
And sure He brought me aid at last!
Woe! unutterable woe to him!
May furies tear him form and limb.
Who shall through malice, envy, hate,
The life of mortal antidate!

Woe to the perjured villain, woe !
May God forever be his foe,
And cast him to some grim abyss
Where famished dragons writhe and hiss,
Who for any cause at all shall dare
Against the innocent to swear !
May he be cursed through endless time,
And ne'er forgiven for his crime !
May his victim from the tomb
Arise, and horrid make his doom !
Flay and shred him, form and soul,
And endless tortures be his goal—
Fell tortures all unknown before,
More dread e'en yet than Furies bore ! "

XII.

He ceased, and on the woman's face
He silent gazed a little space ;
Fell misery, despair and want
Seemed limned upon her visage gaunt ;
A face more foul, illshaped and grim
Had never yet been seen by him !
Black was her eye, and fierce its stare,
And from it shot a fiendish glare ;
And o'er the hellish light they show'd,
Her brows all black and shaggy flow'd !
Her hair was long—nights blackest shade,
And lair on her broad shoulders made ;
Tall was her form, and huge its limb
As is some monster's strong and grim.
Five times she had a mother been,
But scarce her babes that fiend had seen
Than with a knife their lives she shed,
And to wild beasts their bodies fed !

Than her, methinks, all hell could boast
No fiercer fiend 'mongst all its host.

From her grim face, and eyes that burn'd
Like flame in hell, that gazer turn'd
And on George Musgrave fix'd his gaze,
Who lay bewilderd with amaze.
With mournful look he viewed the child,
Then said to him in accents mild:

XIII.

Arise, my boy, and follow me,
For I have come to set you free;
Come, fear from me no slightest harm,
I'll take you to your father's arm!"
Scarce, scarce these words had left his
　　　　tongue
Than fierce at him that woman sprung!
Her fingers swift a pistol clenched—
From his hand the weapon wrenched
As swift as ever lightning grim
Tore from the stately oak a limb;
And as she wrested it from him,
Just as from out his hand it came,
There burst a sound and flash of flame!
And with that flash the pistol's charge
Made through her hand an opening large!
Right through her palm the bullet tore,
And from her hand its centre bore
Then fast from it the crimson blood
Streamed to the floor in ample flood.
Upon the floor the weapon fell,
And from her burst a fearfull yell,
Which echoed through that dismal bield
As if all shrieks from hell had pealed

Together in one fearful blast
Mix'd with all agonies aghast.

XIV.

As scream'd her yell, she backward drew,
On Ragan cast one second's view,
Then swift as light on him she flew,
And round his form her arms she threw;
Around him fix'd her crushing hold,
Strong as an anaconda's fold.
Now, presumptuous fool!" she cried,
With voice that echoed far and wide,
" Your cursed form shall swiftly feel
These arms possess the strength of steel!
And living, you shall pass no more
From out the arms of Ruth Lenore!
Think you to take this boy away,
And not to me his ransom pay?
Not all powers that yet had birth
Within all heaven, hell or earth,
That boy from out my thrall shall free
Till ransom in my hand I see!
But as to you, you worthless fool,
Your heated rashness soon I'll cool,
I'll tear your flesh and crush each bone,
Then food to beasts you shall be thrown."
As thus she speaks, she tighter draws
Her folding arms like dragon's claws,
That own the strength of mountain storm,
Around Earl Ragan's struggling form.

XV.

From side to side he tugged and strain'd,
Yet round his form her arms remain'd!

Still these kept their iron hold,
Nor could he burst from out their fold ;
From side to side his form he threw,
Yet still her fold more stronger grew !
At last awhile they moveless stood,
As two grim statues carved in wood ;
Silent they stood as forms in death,
Save beating heart and panting breath,
Was heard 'mongst them no other sound,
Though tighter still her arms she wound.
Sudden as doth the lion bound
From toils encircling him around,
And fiercely dashes them aside,
Then o'er them stalks with lordly pride,
So, sudden, swift, and with such strength,
He burst from out her fold at length.
With all his force of form and limb,
He scarcely broke the thraldom grim !
And as from out the coil he flew,
He on the floor the woman threw !
With such terrific force she fell,
That fall did all her fury quell !
So still upon the floor she lay,
It seemed all breath had passed away !
Her features ghastly pale and pinched,
Her fingers all convulsive clinched,
Her mouth a gory foam o'erspread,
Streamed nose and ears with liquid red,
And all so still she lay and dead,
It seemed the life from her had fled !
Ne'er a fall so dread she'd known before,
In all her frays with Hugh Lenore,
Nor from his comrades fierce and grim
Of giant strength and thewy limb,

With whom she often in her life,
Had waged unearthly, deadly strife.
A moment's gaze on her he threw,
Then to the trembling boy he drew,
His arms around the lad he cast
And with him o'er the threshold past.
And to'rds his steed from that abode
Through hail and sleet he lightly strode;
In saddle swift his form he threw,
And with the boy through tempests flew.

XVI.

By this the beams of coming day
Had drove the gloom of night away,
Though still did clouds the sky deform
And swept o'er earth the driving storm;
Yet, forth o'er regions drear to view,
That gallant steed with riders flew.
He seem'd to heed nor storm nor hail,
But onward sped like mountain gale;
His form was strong, his limbs were swift
As sands that with the simoom drift;
On he sped o'er many a league,
Nor did he show the least fatigue;
O'er sixty miles his load he bore,
And could have ta'en it sixty more
Before the set of that day's sun,
If such he need that day have done.
And just ere noon he bore his load
Up the steep and slippery road
Along a mountain grim and hoar,
Which led to Richard Musgrave's door;
Here, swift to earth Earl Ragan sprung,
Around the boy his arms he flung;

Right swift he ope'd that mansion's door,
And trod the well-known threshold o'er.

XVII.

Richard Musgrave sat in a chair,
His arms placed on a table near
Which well did books and papers crowd,
And on his hands his head was bowed.
He must have been in slumber sound,
Or wrapt within some thoughts profound
When Ragan ope'd his mansion door
And loudly strode upon the floor,
For raised he not his hoary head,
Though at his side did Ragan tread;
Nor did he stir until the cry,
" Father! Father!" pealed wild and high.
Then from his arms he raised his face,
Which instant met his boy's embrace.
" Kiss me, father! Father, kiss your
        child!"
Loud scream'd the boy with rapture wild,
As round his neck his arms he threw,
And to his lips with kisses grew.
But all so o'erpowered with joy
That parent was, to see his boy,
His arms and tongue he could not move.
The rapture of his soul to prove;
His lips grew pale as those in death,
And thick and heavy came his breath;
And in his cheek, it seem'd the blood
Had turn'd unto a snow-white flood.
But soon the joy that bound his soul,
Like ice that binds the Northern Pole,
Begun to feel the thawing glow
Of love's warm sunshine o'er it flow,

And changed its order of control;
Apace his tears began to roll,
Down his pale cheek they swept amain,
And o'er his offspring flowed like rain ;
At length he shouted hoarse and wild,
" Bless God! God ever bless my child !
Bless him, God, and ever bless the morn,
On which to me this child was born ! "
So spake the father, hoarse with joy,
And to his bosom clasped his boy,
While fast his flowing tears he shed,
O'er him he deem'd till then was dead.

XVIII.

At length he raised his hoary head,
And unto Ragan thus he said :
" Is it a dream, or is it true,
That I my child and Ragan view ?
It was but only yesterday
I saw thee led to cell away—
The horrid murder proved on thee,
Of him who here alive I see !
How comes it now, that you are here ?
Where was my boy, Oh, tell me where ?
Is it the truth, or do I dream ?
It doth to me like fiction seem ;
And fantasies all wild and strange
Throughout my mind and being range,
And visions of eternal change ! "

XIX.

" Why for that murder I was tried,
I cannot tell ! " he swift replied ;
But that your child is safe and well,
You plainly by your eyes can tell.

How it chanced or how it befell
I freed myself from prison cell,
Me to relate to you, I trow,
Is all too long and needless, now ;
Save this, I got from prison free,
As by my coming here you see.
From it I rode through storm and sleet,
Until I did your offspring meet ;
And I believe 'twas God who led
My journey to the dismal shed
Where he was kept in bondage grim,
Until it chanced I rescued him ;
And how it came that he went there,
And who his base abductors were,
And why I'm charged with crime so fell,
I do not know, nor cannot tell!
May be this boy can give some clue
Whereby to pierce this secret through ;
As it is said that truth shall fall
From lips of babes and sucklings small,
And they shall burst through falsehood's
        wall,
Though reared as mountains proud and
        tall!
And innocence and truth, though bare
Of gleaming armor, sword and spear,
Shall over falsehood's might prevail ;
Break all his armor, pierce his mail,
Scatter his might as mist on gale,
And all his lofty strongholds scale ;
From thence disperse his cohorts grim,
However strong of form and limb,
And make them melt as frost away,
When comes the sun's unclouded ray,

And on it pours its warmth amain,
Swift moves it from the hill and plain,
Sends it through lower earth to drain
And never to be seen again.
And this poor boy may burst the vail
Of gloom that doth my soul assail,
Pour in some light so I may see
Through this dense night of mystery!
So unto us now let him tell
All, all that unto him befell,
Since his abductors took him hence—
Tell of his journeys all, and whence."

XX.

GEORGE MUSGRAVE'S STORY:

"'With kite in hand one sunny day,
I did o'er yonder mountain stray,
Which rears aloft its treeless brow
Two miles or more from here. I trow,
So I might let it sail in air
With nought to stop its passage there;
And scarce on high I'd let it fly,
Than near me I did Bolton spy.
"Sonny," he said, "better kite, by far,
Which will fly as high as any star;
Or fly as high as is the moon,
Or is yon glowing sun at noon,
I have at my own home with me,
And I will give it unto thee.
When boy I was, I let it fly
Till I could see it touch the sky!
I oft have let it pass through cloud
Where lightnings flashed with thunders
        loud,

And then I've drawn it down to me,
And lightning bolts would on it see!
I took them off and sent it back
To fly upon the thunder's track,
And when of bolts it gathered more,
I'd do as I had done before—
I'd pull it down with all its load,
And them within my pockets stowed!
And oh, these bolts, are fair to see—
Like starry gems they glitter free!
Lots, lots of them are home with me,
And them with kite, I'll give to thee!
I just am on my way to'rds home,
If thither there with me thou'lt roam,
I'll give them all to thee, my son,
And with them thou'lt have lots of fun!
It is not far for thee to go,
Thou'lt be back in an hour or so.
So come along, my son, with me,
And thine the kite and gems shall be."

XXI.

That with him I went, I scarce need tell,
For this you know but all too well.
I roam'd with him o'er lofty fell,
O'er wild morass, through wooded dell,
Until we reached a lonely bield
That was midst brush and vines concealed;
So hid by them you could not trace
A rood away there was such place.
We reached the hut, he ope'd the door,
But as I trod the threshold o'er,
I saw three men stretched on the floor,
And mongst them him call'd Hugh Lenore;

All dead drunk, were they, I ween,
For cans of grog were near them seen,
And from the floor they did not rise,
Nor stir at all, nor ope their eyes,
Although loud noise old Bolton made
As there each sleeper he surveyed,
And hoarsely said, "What! drunk so
    soon?
Why, damn it! it is scarcely noon!
You must right jolly times have seen,
While I have been away, I ween."
As this he said, a can he caught
Within his hand, and it he brought
Unto his mouth; a lively smile
Displayed o'er all his face the while;
Long drank he from the spacious can,
Then said to me, "My little man,
When more advanced in years you grow,
I guess you, too, will also know
The joy, the ecstacy, and bliss,
In drinking luscious grog like this!
It makes a mortal feel sublime!
And you this truth will learn in time."

XXII.

An hour past, and that old man,
Again, again, drank from the can.
Until a score of times, I ween,
That can unto his mouth had been!
Between each drink he'd say to me.
" I soon will give the kite to thee,
And pocket full of thunderbolts,
Bright as the eyes of tricky colts,
Long ropes of bright and flashing gems,
In clusters thick as grapes on stems;

And I will homeward go with thee,
Thou to thy father's door will see."

XXIII.

Time past, and with a heavy snore.
From out his sleep rose Hugh Lenore ;
Around the hut his gaze he cast,
Then rose, and out the hut he past ;
Strode from the bield a little space,
And with him Bolton left the place.
They paused, I saw them where they stood.
Though well hid were they by viny wood,
And thus I heard old Bolton say :
" I got an easy job to-day ;
Down wants it done, and Crawford too.
'Twas them who gave it me to do ;
They wish that boy put out the way.
And want it done this very day ·
So I am going him to slay,
For they will give most ample pay.
To do the job I've ta'en my oath,
And do it so 'twill serve them both—
To make it plain to you in words,
I with one stone must kill two birds.
Within the way this youngster stands
Of Judge Down heiring Musgrave's lands ;
So I must put him out the way,
And let Judge Down o'er these gain sway :
For in the mother's will is found
Some clause which just like this doth
　　sound :—
" If dies my child before he's grown.
Or has the years of manhood known—
Say twenty years have o'er him flown.
My brother all my wealth shall own."

So when I put him out the way,
You see the Judge will have full sway.
Concerned in it is Crawford, too,
For Logan's maid he cannot woo,
Nor can he hope to win her hand
While Ragan in the way doth stand,
Which causes Crawford much of woe;
Then I must kill this stripling so
'Twill plainly seem through coming time
That it was Ragan did the crime!
So he will soon in cell be flung,
Be tried, condemned, and for it hung!
On Crawford's way to Mary's love.
No Ragan shall a hindrance shove.
But be free as that of the dove
That flaps its wings in air above!
Without making it a lengthy yarn,
The rents in Crawford's love I'll darn,
And put it on a stepping sarn.
There is a lofty, craggy carn,
That overlooks a gurge and tarn
Right closely seen by Ragan's barn
And thither I the boy will bring.
All, all his clothes from him I'll wring,
Stain o'er his clothing with his blood,
Then cast him in the whirlpool's flood;
I'll place his robes in Ragan's mow.
Just where they will be found, I trow;
Then straight I'll noise it far and wide.
By Ragan's hand George Musgrave died;
Swear that I saw him do the deed;
But help in this I'll surely need,
So you must swear the same as me,
Just make your tale with mine agree;

And lots of boys we'll bring to swear,
And prove the crime on Ragan clear;
In prison cell he must be flung,
Be tried, convicted, also hung.
Then lots of grog, we'll have, old boy,
And grog, you know, brings lots of joy."

XXIV.

" I'll help you through," the other said,
" For this, I pledge my life and head!
I'm on my road to Ragan's now
And if you will it so allow,
I'll do for you this little task,
And for the job no mite I'll ask !
'Twill save you going there to day,
And long and weary is the way ;
So if it with your wishes be
Just send the boy along with me ;
In doing it I'll take a pride ! "
" I will," the other swift replied.
And me from out the hut he called ;
I was not by their talk appall'd ;
For something in me seemed to say,
I from these men would get away ;
So with no sign of fright nor fear,
I to those ruffians drew me near.
To speak old Bolton thus began :
" Now, you, my noble little man,
Just go along with this, my friend ;
Not far with him you'll have to wend ;
A bow he'll give of hickory strong,
And lots of arrows sharp and long ;
A bow that sends a shaft more swift
Than e'er did sand on tempest drift ;

A bow that sends an arrow far,
And straight into the furthest star !
When this he gives to you, my son.
Just back to me right swiftly run;
I'll have your kite all ready then,
And bolts ta'en from the lightning's den
Where thunders growl and roll and burn ;
Now go, and swiftly back return."

XXV.

Across the mountains, wild and hoar,
I strode along with Hugh Lenore ;
Soon roam'd we through a narrow pass,
Which open'd on a wide morass ;
Across this wild and dismal fen
With weary feet I journeyed then ;
The place seem'd filled with snakes and
    frogs,
With lizards, and with snorting hogs,
With rank, coarse grass and rotten logs ;
And right glad was I when it we past,
And trod on solid ground at last !
For shades of night were round us cast,
And everything looked drear and ghast ;
For clouds of huge and ragged form,
And edges all with lightning warm,
Commenced athwart the sky to swarm,
And showing signs of coming storm.
We gained a forest dense and drear—
Huge vines o'er trees were growing there,
But ere a mile through this we strode,
We came upon a lone abode—
As dismal and as grim a bield,
As e'er from storm gave mortal shield

In any dreary bog or moor,
And 'twas the home of Hugh Lenore.
Within his hand the latch he caught,
And swift the door wide open brought;
We enterd, and save Ruth Lenore,
Of mortal kind I saw no more.

XXVI.

Soon with choice food she spread the
    board,
And well my plate with dainties stored,
And at that meal, if truth I'd tell,
I'd say they used me kind and well;
The woman spoke right mild to me
And said, henceforth her son I'd be.
Soon as my hungry mood they fed,
They put me in a cozy bed;
Soon sound asleep I seemed to lie,
But wide awake the while was I!
Both lightly to my bedside drew,
And o'er me cast a lengthy view;
But ere away from me they stept,
Thy deemed that I most soundly slept.

XXVII.

That sound I slept they had no doubt,
Away they sped, the lamp blew out,
And unto bed they also drew,
Their forms upon the couch they threw.
Long time they silent lay; no word
From either one of them I heard;
At length to whispering they drew,
Soon this more loud and louder grew,
Till I could plainly hear at last
Each syllable that 'tween them past.

" Yes," said Lenore, " the truth to tell,
I have deceived old Bolton well!
Ere this, he thinks, the boy is dead,
His life-blood o'er his clothing shed ;
His body cast within the tarn,
And gory robes in Ragan's barn.
But let the old fool fancy so,
The truth would only cause him woe.
On Ragan we will cast the crime,
And swear to it when comes the time ;
And when on him we've proved the deed,
And Down and Crawford pay its meed,
Then I will straight to Musgrave tell
His boy is safe, alive and well ;
And if he will my toil reward,
To him shall be the child restored.
Soon as such news to him be told,
He'll give me gold ! he'll give me gold !
And doing thus, old girl, you see,
I'll coin, I'll make a double fee !
And you and me ! and you and me !
Right jolly times through life shall see ! ' "

XXVIII.

What else he said, I could not hear,
For thunder peals benumbed mine ear,
Without the tempest howl'd and roar'd,
And down the rain in torrents poured ;
The lightning flashed, the thunder peal'd
And shook all o'er that dismal bield ;
And lull'd to sleep by screaming blast,
Into the land of dreams I pass'd.

XXIX.

I wakened in the early dawn,
Just as gray tints o'er skies were drawn,
Long ere the sky was rosy red,
I woke and sprung me forth from bed;
But as from out of bed I drew,
These clothes to me the woman threw;
And said to me, " My boy, wear them,
Your others I must darn and hem."
I donn'd the garb, and cross'd the floor
To where wide open stood the door,
And there without I saw Lenore,
With vessel full of clotted gore—
An earthen vessel, long and deep,
And near him lay a slaughtered sheep;
I saw him take the clothes I wore
And steep them in that tub of gore!
Scarce a sight of this I caught,
Than me from there the woman brought;
Fiercely she closed that shanty's door,
Bade me ne'er look that threshold o'er;
From that morn till now, I've no more
Gazed on the face of Hugh Lenore.
What time with her I sojourned there.
She always gave me best of fare;
Whate'er of her I chanced to crave,
To me with ready hand she gave.
But on the night that you came there,
I longed and yearned to journey here;
And when I thought that woman slept,
All noiseless from my bed I crept,
And light as air unto the door
I pass'd along that shanty's floor;

Nigh all the bolts I had unbarr'd,
When one against the staple jarr'd,
Which roused the woman from her sleep,
Who did on me like tigress leap!
A storm of oathes she on me threw,
As to my trembling form she flew,
Upon my head she dealt a blow,
And me upon the floor did throw,
And there I lay as still as death,
Almost afraid to draw my breath,
Until you trod her threshold o'er
And found me lying on the floor.' "

XXX.

Here ceased the boy; his tale was told,
And Ragan's mysteries unrolled,
Grim darkness left each tangled fold,
And he could plainly all behold!
" Can it indeed be true," he thought,
" That Crawford has this evil wrought?
On me such shame and trouble brought?
Of wrong I've never done him aught!
And wealth I oft have loaned him much,
When I scarcely could spare him such.
I've always deem'd that man my friend,
And one on whom I might depend,
If ever trouble grim and sore
Should chance to knock upon my door.
Yes, pure and bright, I deem'd his soul,
As any star that gilds the pole;
Firm as the rock by ocean found,
Deep bedded on the solid ground,
That neither storm nor wave can move,
However fierce their fury prove!

Is it a dream ? or did my ear
But now that stripling's story hear?
Am I indeed, deceived, betrayed,
By one in whom all trust I laid ?
And one who aye professed to be
The warmest, truest friend to me ?
Can it be true a soul so grim,
And heart so base is found in him ?
Oh, life of man indeed is strange,
And we will find it full of change
Where'er upon this world we range !
E'en though we roam through joy and
     mirth,
Or where has only sorrow birth ;
It matters not the slightest where,
All, all, is ever changing here ;
Forever shifting as the sand
The tempest moves o'er desert land,
Where naught a moment's space of time
Remains the same, through all its clime.

XXXI.

Oh, that the eye of mortal man,
Could only through the future scan !
Could pierce the gloom around it cast,
And see it as he can the past!
How many troubles would we shun,
And dangers into which we run !
We do not pause to look nor think,
But tread fondly by the mossy brink
Of some tremendous wall of carn,
Which overlooks dark, awful tarn,
Whose sable, silent floods below
Sweep on where distant whirlpools flow,

And carries with resistless force,
All things it meets upon its course.
Down from the mossy brink we go
All unawares, to floods below,
Are borne upon its current fast,
And in its roaring vortex cast;
Are lost amidst its foaming flow,
And spin to its abyss below,
Where, far beneath its horrid rim,
Amidst its regions dark and grim,
Dread, awful things of form and limb
Amidst the roaring eddies swim.

XXXII.

Perhaps e'en now I stand betrayed
By others in whom trust I've laid,
For whom, if fate had will'd it so,
I would have braved all mortal woe!
Yes, willingly have met my grave,
If them from woe and harm I'd save;
Whose love I deem'd was true to me,
As is the flood that fills the sea,
Which naught shall wholly waste away
Till time and nature shall decay;
But over all its bed shall flow,
Hide its unevenness below,
And not one imperfection show,
Though wild its waves the tempests throw.
Yes, just to me as faithful prove,
And by my side forever move.
Hide, hide all faults within me found,
Though did they numberless abound!
Perhaps e'en Mary Logan, now,
Would meet me with disdainful brow;

Perhaps e'en at this very time
She deems me guilty of the crime!
Yea, deems me as the basest wretch,
Whose neck did ever gallows stretch!
And Crawford Storm had never sought
To bring on me the stain he brought,
Had he not seen within that maid
Some signs of love for him displayed;
Saw that the love that for me burn'd,
Could easy unto him be turn'd;
I could be readily dethron'd,
And banished from the realm I own'd!
Perhaps e'en now her soul is free
Of far less scorn for him than me;
And never near her shall I move,
Till fate to me this fact shall prove!"

XXXIII.

While thus his aching thoughts revolved,
O'er problems which they might have solv'd
As easy as the noonday sun
Makes frost-work into liquid run,
When on a warm, bright summer's day
The frost-work comes beneath its ray,
Had he but chose to wend his way
Within the presence of that maid.
A hand was on his shoulder laid,
And brought him from each gloomy
    thought,
With which profound his mind was fraught,
And spake a voice he knew fullwell—
" I went to free you from your cell,
But found that you had gone away,
And I have searched for you all day,

Hoping that we would somewhere meet,
Amidst this storm of hail and sleet;
For Ellen Fay revealed to me
The secret that she set you free;
And said, none, none your flight would know
Until at least three days should go;
And as I homeward bent my way,
I fancied we would meet to-day.
And for this I fondly prayed,
Though 'tis by chance that here I strayed."
Earl Ragan swiftly turned around,
So wrapp'd he'd been in thought profound
He had not seen the door thrown wide,
And o'er it's threshold Logan stride;
But as he turned to meet the clasp
Of Logan in his stalwart grasp,
He said, " There, alive, is the boy,
Whose life they swore I did destroy!"
" Where ? " said Logan.
                              Earl Ragan turned,
But nowhere he the child descerned.
So wrapp'd in thought had Ragan been,
He had not the departure seen
Of Richard Musgrave and his boy
From out that room, who, wild with joy,
Had left to let his household know
They had no longer cause for woe;
That they had mourned and wept with him
Till hearts were broke and eyes were dim,
For one alive and sound in limb,
Not murdered horrible and grim,
And cast away forevermore
From them, where hidden whirlpools roar,
Swift to grim caves their waters pour,
And such will do till time is o'er.

PART V.

I.

A starless night, and piercing cold,
For ice lay thick o'er hill and wold ;
Roar'd hoarse and loud the driving blast,
While sleet from inky clouds was cast!
Hard, thick and fast the frozen rain
The clouds poured on the earth amain ;
And through the gloom and tempest wild,
Ragan, Logan, Musgrave and his child,
Well armed and on their chargers fleet,
Set out in spite of storm and sleet
To noise the joyous tidings round
To friends and foes, wherever found,
The child was safe, alive and well!
And let him them his story tell ;
And wipe each gory stain away,
That o'er the name of Ragan lay !
Yes, show alike to friend and foe,
They could no stain on Ragan throw !
And muster all the neighbors round,
That yet were true to Ragan found—
Arouse the neighbors, one and all
O'er moor and plain and mountain tall,
As though they heard an earthquake's
      sound,
Uprooting fierce the solid ground,
And shaking all the country round !
Make them come forth all undismayed,
And gather fast to Ragan's aid !—

Rally, not only for his cause,
But broken and insulted laws!
A vigilance committee form—
Straight seize Judge Down and Crawford
    Storm!
Those villains, Bolton and Lenore,
And all who, 'gainst him falsely swore!
Bring perjured scoundrels to account,
And for such crimes the gallows mount!
"For," said John Logan, "those who bear
False witness—unto such will swear,
Should be for life in dungeon flung,
Or unto death on gallows hung!—
Should meet no milder doom than him
Who has committed murder grim!
And as some mighty avalanche,
That breaks the forests, bole and branch,
And leaves their broken roots upturned,
Far from their native mountains spurn'd,
Amidst the roaring floods below—
Where they no more shall vintage show,
So shall we, on those villains go,
And deal to them eternal woe!
Or give them dungeon, ball and chain!
We'll drive them from the land amain;
Their rule and reign shall soon be o'er,
Such fiends shall curse the land no more!"

II.

Such words in wrath John Logan said,
And forth upon such errand sped,
In spite of driving storm and blast,
And sleet that showered hard and fast;
Away they sped o'er hill and wold,
Unchecked by gloom or piercing cold.

Many a house that night they sought
And from their beds the inmates brought
So they might all the boy behold,
And hear the story that he told.
Soon as each neighbor saw the boy,
All wild was their suprise and joy—
Cried " Vengeance, on the wretches grim.
May furies crush them form and limb!
Who were so base and vile and low,
To such a crime on Ragan throw!"
" Now, friends and neighbors," Logan said.
" Upon each cursed villain's head,
Who in this plot Judge Down has led,
Must fall a retribution dread!
So do not sleep at all to night,
But forth like us, now, take your flight
In spite of storm and pelting hail,
Rouse our friends o'er hill and dale;
Fly! rouse them up on field and wold,
Wherever you a house behold!
Awake all people, far and wide,
Tell them to rally to my side;
Reck not how fierce the tempests roam,
But straight to come to Logan's home!
To meet him there ere dawn of day,
And let us speed in vast array
Upon those dens of grimest crime,
Ere to escape we give them time."

III.

Away, away, through storm and sleet;
Away, away, on chargers fleet!
O'er field and wold, o'er hill and vale,
The neighbors rode to spread the tale.

From house to house the news was spread
Swift as could swiftest chargers tread !
Voice after voice took up the tale,
Until it rung o'er hill and dale !
Till over field and wold it past
Swift as the pinions of the blast;
And long ere earth had cast away
The robes of night, donn'd those of day.
Had met a formidable throng
Of Grangers, active tall and strong,
Who, to avenge Earl Ragan's wrong,
To'rds Logan's mansion sped along—
Who not for either quick or dead
Would from the path of justice tread.

IV.

Upon a dark and winding road
Three miles or more from his abode.
Along which groves of cedars grew
And much obscure all things from view.
Though shelter gave from storms that
            blew,
John Logan and his comrades drew.
Two hundred yards from him ahead,
On the winding road, Earl Ragan led;
Loose rein and spur he gave his steed,
For soon, he knew that path would lead.
And bring him to Logan's abode ;
For this sole cause ahead he rode.
With yearning heart and joyous mind,
And left his comrades far behind ;
For first of them he wished to be.
To tell his Mary he was free
Of all the crime upon him thrown.
Let this to her by him be known.

When sudden on his pathway drew
A horse and rider, right in view,
And straight a woman's scream he heard.
Which o'er the roar of tempest stirr'd !
And as that horseman nearer drew—
Still plainer came within his view—
A woman's form he soon espied,
Did with the man the charger ride ;
The steed both man and woman bore ;
A sable robe the female wore,
And sat the bow of saddle o'er—
The man behind and she before ;
His arms were round the woman cast.
And just as they beside him past.
Another scream the woman gave,
And cried, Oh, me ! for God's sake save !

V.

" Halt ! halt ! " Earl Ragan fiercely cried,
Just as they darted by his side ;
And strove to catch their flying rein,
But only strove to catch in vain !
On, on, by him they lightly flew,
As swift as ever tempest blew,
And still her shrieks the woman gave,
And cries of Pity me, and save !
Which rose above the roar of blast ;
But scarce five yards by him they past.
Than straight his hand a pistol caught.
Its aim upon the steed he brought,
A flash of bright and ruddy flame,
From out the hand of Ragan came.
And with it burst a sharp, loud sound.
And swift the steed dropped on the ground.

The charger gave one piercing groan.
As there he on the earth was thrown.

VI.

As flies the bird from fowler's snare,
And wings its flight to distant air,
And safely hides midst brush or weed,
So, swift and with such lightning speed
The rider of that tumbled steed,
His feet from out the stirrups freed.
And midst the grove of cedars flew.
That all around so densely grew,
And straight was lost to Ragan's view.
Swift from his steed his form he threw,
And to that woman's rescue drew.
Then, then that female form he knew!

VII.

'Twere long and needless now to tell.
All, all that there that night befell,
When Logan and the rest drew round,
And in this plight his Mary found!
And by her saw the dying steed
From which she had just thus been freed!
These facts to them she soon made clear :
The villain who had brought her there
Was none but Bolton, well they knew,
From his description, which she drew :
Early that morning he had strode,
As beggar unto their abode ;
He'd craved for bread ; she'd given food
And satisfied his hungry mood ;
He'd craved God's blessing on her head,
For having him so kindly fed ;

A holy ditty then he sung,
And left with mild and civil tongue.
When night closed in again he came,
And this time called her by her name,
Then said, " Your father and a friend
Bade me right swiftly to you wend,
And bid you not a moment waste,
But straight away unto them haste !
But here, this letter will reveal
All that they did from me conceal ;
'Twill tell you what of you they crave."
A letter unto me he gave ;
It swift unto a lamp I bore,
Then straight the cover open tore
And read the writing o'er and o'er— .
From end to end, three times or more !
That my own father's hand had penn'd
That letter all from end to end,
I had no slightest doubt the while,
For all was penn'd within his style ;
Each letter on the scroll surveyed,
I would have sworn my father made !
His style the writing nothing lack'd,
'Twas shaped and framed his way exact.
I swiftly glanced the writing o'er,
This was the message that it bore :

VIII.

" Dear daughter, come to me with speed ;
He who brings this the way will lead.
This morn I found I could not bail
By gold, Earl Ragan out of jail,
By force of arm I got him free,
And have him here all safe with me.

But much I fear when it is known
That he has from his dungeon flown,
The Sheriff's men will follow him,
And sure his fate will be most grim;
If they should capture him to-night,
He would not see the morning's light;
They'd hang him on the nearest tree,
He'd from them none of mercy see!
For such a fate I too much fear
To let him in my house appear;
The Sheriff's men may find him there;
But you can safely journey here;
Come with this messenger in haste,
And do not now a moment waste.
Hark, daughter, unto what I say,
Your loving father's words obey;
Do not a moment's space delay,
But come, this man will lead the way.
But let of this no single word
By any in the house be heard,
When read, this in the fire throw,
Where it shall straight to ashes go;
And do not let the servants know
Away you have been summoned so;
Keep all as secret as the grave,
And we may yet Earl Ragan save."

IX.

That it was forged I never dream'd,
It all so like my father's seem'd,
It came from him I well believed,
Nor had one thought I was deceived.
Soon as I had the letter conn'd,
My cloak and hood I swiftly donn'd,

To shield me from the tempest keen,
And by the servants all unseen
I with him pass'd the threshold o'er,
Unheard by all I locked the door,
Then forth through night and pelting hail,
And through the roaring, sweeping gale,
I followed where that villain led.
Till many a weary step I'd sped;
At length we reached a clump of wood
That swaying to the tempest stood;
Amongst it pines and cedars grew,
Which hid all things within from view;
Within it swift we onward drew,
For where he led I did pursue.
But scarcely twenty yards we'd past
Amidst the gloom it round us cast.
Than I a saddled steed espied,
And two men standing by his side.
As to that steed my leader drew,
His form upon the horse he threw.
" Now hand her up, my boys!" he cried,
To those two men that there I spied.
" This maid is Crawford's promised bride,
And I shall bear her to his side!"
Then me they seized with all their force,
And bore me struggling on the horse:
My form upon the steed they threw,
Round me his arms the horseman drew
And said, " Be still my pretty maid.
Of me you need not be afraid!
You must not show the least alarms,
For you are safe within my arms;
To cry there is no use at all,
It will not free you from my thrall;

Just go along right still with me,
And you shall shortly Crawford see !
For fitter spouse for you is he,
Than Ragan, though of crime all free :
But if a noise you dare to make,
I will your pretty jaw bones break ;
I'll tie your hands and split your tongue,
And in some flood you shall be flung !
So scream not, while you go with me,
Or what I've said, I wean, you'll see ! "

X.

As this he said with savage tone,
That thrill'd through marrow, nerve and
  bone,
Within the startled charger's flank,
Sudden and deep his rowel sank :
And down the road of crashing sleet,
Thundered his charger's flying feet.
And terrorstricken and dismayed,
Then, then, I knew I was betrayed !
As down the winding road we drew,
Until we came within your view ! ' "

XI.

'Twere vain for me to limn or tell,
The rage that did in Logan swell ;
Through all his form the bounding blood
Went sweeping like a mountain flood ;
His heart was throbbing in his breast
Like some fierce ocean in unrest,
And plainly could be heard its sound
As beating gainst its walls around, ·

As if that broad and ample chest
Gave not scope unto its fierce unrest;
For anger seem'd to shake his form,
As tree that swayes in mountain storm;
Rage lit his eye and dyed his cheek,
And fill'd him so he scarce could speak.
Within his arms he clasped his child,
And thus broke forth in accents wild:

XII.

" Curst be the fiend who brought you here,
And laid for you this cunning snare!
On him shall fall a father's curse,
And what to him shall be far worse,
On him shall fall that father's hand,
And lifeless crush him in the sand!
Yea, I shall crush him unto death!
By my own hand shall cease his breath!"

XIII.

As this he said, away he flew
Where dense the grove of cedars grew,
And long he midst the forest sought,
But he no trace of Bolton caught,
Although he searched it far and wide.
" Father, come back," the maiden cried;
Homeward bear my shivering form
From out this driving hail and storm!
Come, father, pity take on me,
And set me from this tempest free!
Father, dear father, come away!
Dear father, list to what I say!"
The tempest roared so hoarse and wild,
The father did not hear his child,

As mongst those frozen trees he sought
For one he would have gladly caught,
And dealt on him all hurt and harm
That slumbered in his stalwart arm ;
But as amongst the trees he wound
And trod upon the sleety ground,
His feet kept up such crashing sound,
His daughter's cries and shouts were
    drown'd ;
And not till those who with him sought
Were with the fruitless task o'erwraught,
Did he regain his daughter's side
And with her towards his mansion ride ;
But ere they left the dismal place,
A smile was limned on every face,
For shouted loud George Musgrave there,
So that if Bolton anywhere
Was crouching midst that forest drear,
He could his voice right plainly hear.
" Say, Bolton ! " loud the stripling cried,
" By Hugh Lenore I have not died !
So all your thunderbolts and kite,
You straight can bring to me to-night !
If ever to a man I grow,
And fate you in my path shall throw,
I'll tell you plainly then, you lied !
None of my feelings from you hide."
Thus spake the boy, who little knew
In Bolton's ear his shouting flew ;
And also every word he spake
Did on the ear of Crawford break ;
For he was close beside them there,
And all they spake did plainly hear :
He lay to them so close, so near,
Amidst the cedars dark and drear,

Which dense around did foliage rear,
Each word they spake fell on his ear;
And twice beside the place he lay
Amidst the cedar's sable spray,
Both Ragan and John Logan past,
But not on him their vision cast.

XIV.

With speed they left the dismal place,
Where only cedars they could trace,
That shook to tempests to and fro,
And round did icy branches show;
Where naught they deemed they'd left be-
    hind
In shape of any breathing kind,
Save dying steed that groaning lay
And slowly bled his life away;
A noble steed as ever trod
O'er solid rock or dewy sod,
As ever grazed o'er pastures green,
Or mongst the race of steeds was seen;
With thewy limbs and brawny form,
Fleet as the blast, strong as the storm;
With neck that looked like bended bow,
And mane that hung in heavy flow;
With stately head, erect and proud,
And eyes that flashed like flame in cloud;
Ears forward pricked as though to hear
Some sound to which he journeyed near;
From some strange object that he eyed
With snorting nostrils huge and wide;
With shoulders deep, and brawny breast,
Which plain his matchless strength con-
    fess'd.

John Logan and his daughter rode
With tempest's speed to their abode,
In spite of gloom and driving storm;
One arm was twined around her form,
And 'gainst his broad and swelling breast
She placed her gentle head at rest.

XV.

" Daughter," he said, " to-night I see
That God has not abandoned me!
That He doth still beside me stay,
And ever guides me on my way;
Prospers my ways where'er I move,
And still a friend to me doth prove;
And will not let the evil arm
Deal me or mine a lasting harm;
And lightly turns aside the blow
Was meant to cause my overthrow.
And were I in the whirlpool's flow,
Where waters spin to depths below,
He would not let me downward go
But straight to me would mercy show;
Yea, me he would not fail to save,
And draw from out the whelming wave.
It is not oft I go this way,
By either night-time or by day,
'Tis only when the sun is warm,
Or sweeps like now a piercing storm,
That I this woody high-road take,
Then it is done for shelter's sake;
I alway take some other road,
When I go forth from my abode,
Or unto it I wend my way,
Let it be either night or day;

And when on it my charger strode
I felt like turning off this road
And guiding him another way,
But go it, something seemed to say!
Though it was all against my will
I rode along this woody hill;
I drew my rein, and let my steed
Move up the slope with slackened speed;
I let the rest ride on before,
, While in my mind I pondered o'er
The voice I heard within me say
John Logan you must take this way!
And while this fill'd my spirit all,
Kept it close bound in pensive thrall,
I heard your voice for mercy call,
Heard pistols blare, and something fall.
Now, child, I know 'twas God who spake.
Bade me this dismal passage take;
None other voice than his I heard,
His was the whisper in me stirr'd!
His was the hand that drew the rein,
And forced me up this road amain;
His was the arm that rescued you
From that vile fiend of hellish crew;
Your rescue, child, God will'd and plann'd,
And had it done by Ragan's hand.

XVI.

Thus as he spake, they onward drew
Until the mansion rose in view;
But scarce within the yard they came,
Than round them flashed a ruddy flame,
That from some score of lanterns gleam'd,
And far on night their lustre stream'd;

All Logan's servants, young and old,
Did in their hands a lantern hold ;
They just had missed the lovely maid,
And for her safety all afraid,
They'd searched the mansion through and
      through,
But nowhere she had met their view !
The door was locked, the key had flown,
Out, the lamps that were lit were blown
Within the room she last had stood,
And vanished were her cloak and hood ;
So at her absence all dismayed,
Their numbers swiftly they arrayed,
And forth they flew through storm and
      cold
To search for her o'er field and wold,
Through valley and through mountain cave.

XVII.

Wild were the shouts of joy they gave,
High o'er the roar of storms they grew !
And on their wings o'er mountains flew,
When Logan and his daughter drew
And followers within their view,
When there the boy before them sped,
Whom they till then had fancied dead,
And Ragan, too, their eyes beheld,
Hoarse, high, their shouts on tempest
      swell'd ;
True, heart-felt joy flash'd in their eyes,
And fill'd their souls with glad surprise ;
Their lanterns swift on earth they plac'd
And did to every horseman haste,
The reins within their hands they caught,
And from each steed each rider brought ;

And while upon the tempest roar'd
The deafening welcome that they pour'd,
Within their arms each form they bore
The threshold of the mansion o'er;
The lamps were lit, and flamed each hearth
Midst shouts of heartfelt joy and mirth.

XVIII.

To stable were the horses led,
And if e'er steeds were amply fed,
Had corn and hay before them spread.
And given dry and easy bed,
And wiped of every drop of rain
That on them lay, from feet to mane,
These weary steeds received it there!
But well did Ragan's charger fare,
To it they showed especial care!
They viewed it with delighted eyes,
Praised long its thewy limbs and size,
And all agreed a nobler steed
They never yet had given feed!
This thought seem'd firmly in them set,
Its lord would be their master, yet.

XIX.

Bright shone the lights in Logan's home,
In ample mugs the ale did foam,
In goblets bright and deep and broad,
The ruddy sparkling wine was pour'd;
With ample fare the board was crown'd
The best within the country found;
Fish, flesh and fowl, were smoking there,
The best of earth or flood or air,
Upon that ample table stood;
The wine look'd tempting, rich and good,

Right luscious look'd the ale and food,
And round it throng'd in hungry mood
Five happy souls, as void of care,
As ever trod this planet here;
For those they loved upon this sphere
The most of all were with them there!
One ate and drank with teeming joy
Near his feasting, chatting boy;
One as he drank and ate, the while
Did on his lovely daughter smile,
Whose beaming brow and rosy face
Displayed each sweetest charm and grace
That God e'er gave to woman's race
Since first on earth he did her place,
When He the glorious creature wrought,
First unto life the seraph brought
And her fair form and being fraught
With all the noblest charms He caught
Midst boundless regions of His thought,
And how to blend, divinely taught;
From things the best within His span
He did that creature mould and plan;
And placed her here to bless or ban
The race he loved and christened man.
The other ate and drank beside
His all beauteous, promised bride,
And as he sat beside the maid
And her bewitching face surveyed,
He felt that God had him repaid
For woes that fate had round him laid;
And thanks to God swept through his
        soul
For peace and joy did it control.
Loud roar'd without the tempest's din,
But all was feasting mirth within,

'Mongst souls untouched by crime or sin.
And souls where such no hold shall win.

XX.

When they had left the dying steed,
And that lone place of them was freed,
Had far upon their journey sped,
No more was heard their horses' tread,
From out his dismal hiding place
Old Bolton moved with lively pace.
And trod along the sleety road,
Which brought him soon to his abode;
Where his two aids had swiftly sped,
Through short cuts o'er the mountain's
        head—
Lone byways known but to a few,
Which to that dismal shanty drew.
These, these they threaded, nimbly traced.
When on the steed they'd Mary placed.
And left her to old Bolton's care;
But where to go, they reck'd not where.
With curse and groan at fate and God,
O'er sleety paths old Bolton trod;
On, on, he sped till Crawford's ear
His footfalls could no longer hear,
Till on the crisp and brittley sleet,
Was heard no crashing from his feet;
Then from a cedar huge and tall
Whose spray was black as midnight's pall,
And dense as is the clouds of night,
Whose fold hides all the moon from sight
Crawford Storm down swiftly drew,
From of his robes the sleet he threw,
And towards the dying steed he sped,
With padded feet and noiseless tread;

Beside the fallen steed he drew,
O'er it cast a lingering view
With eyes that flashed with fiendish glow;
And with fierce curse and kick and blow,
He strove to make that charger rise,
But vain the task, on earth he lies
In spite of curse and kick and blow,
While from his wound in rapid flow
The blood pours out, and crimson glow
Doth to the frozen sleet bestow;
Save groans that tell his pain and woe,
No signs of life that steed doth show.

XXI.

As lightnings flash in sable skies,
And flame on high incessant flies,
So blazed the rage in Crawford's eyes
When he'd proved the courser could not
    rise.
And thus he muttered, fierce and low,
" May fate deal everlasting woe
On that cursed wretch who dealt the blow
That caused my charger's overthrow!
May fate discard him evermore,
Deal him all throes this charger bore!
For this to me he owes a debt
That he shall trebly pay me yet,
In spite of all the force of fate,
And all the fraud of love and hate,
Of life, and grisly death, its mate!
The time will come yet, soon or late,
That cursed Ragan yet shall cower,
A 'fenceless victim in my power;
He yet shall meet an end most grim,
Though periled be my life and limb

In the attempt to injure him;
Though I through seething lava swim,
I do not care, I shall not reck,
So that the gallows stretch his neck!
And Bolton, curse his tricky soul.
I'll deal on him eternal dole!
Him death shall also shortly woo,
Shall win and wed and mate him, too!
Bolton in whom such trust I laid;
Me, me, that traitor has betrayed!
To me he has most grossly lied,
By him George Musgrave never died!
From home he's only him decoyed.
His life, his life, he ne'er destroyed!
In him I trusted and believed,
And me, and me, he has deceived!
Yes, yes, to me he's grossly lied,
Has me betrayed on every side!
But for his treachery, his breath
Shall forfeit pay to me and death!
He soon shall die most dread and grim
With agony in every limb!"

XXII.

With curses dropping from his tongue
As dread and grim as ever rung
On breath pour'd out by human tongue.
From that lone dying steed he sprung;
And swiftly strode the sleety road
Which led to Bolton's drear abode;
He sped upon the shortest way
That 'tween him and the shanty lay;
As lonely path as ever seen,
Which few could walk, save him, I ween;

A full long mile he had to pass
O'er hill, vale, bush and wild morass,
Ere he would reach the dismal bield
That did from storms old Bolton shield;
But o'er this mile he swiftly sped,
And did in Bolton's shanty tread.
Some huge pine logs blazed on the hearth,
Save these the hut of light was dearth;
These threw around a gloomy light,
And left the place half hid in night.
Upon the dirty, filthy floor
Stretched out the burning logs before,
Just light enough to show each face,
Lay the three inmates of the place—
Bolton, and Joe, and Bill—the three
We did within it lately see.
But soon as Crawford ope'd the door,
Ere he had cross'd the threshold o'er.
Old Bolton leapt from off the floor.
For him placed a chair the hearth before,
Bow'd low his head, and humbly said,
" Boss, welcome to old Bolton's shed !
A fearful night is this, I trow,
For you to be out walking, now.
Boss, our fire is very low,
But for your sake, shall brighter glow !
So take this chair, now, if you please,
Here you can warm yourself at ease."

XXIII.

As this he said, some chips he threw
Amongst the blazing logs, and blew
On them until the hearth became
One roaring blaze of ruddy flame,

Which sparks in blasts sent up the flue
Unnumbered sparks of ruddy hue,
While Crawford, in the proffered chair
Sat down in calm, familiar air.
Serene his visage looked the while,
In fact, o'er it was limned a smile;
No sign the while at all he show'd
Of the fell rage that in him glow'd,
Nor of the savage vengeance grim
That throbb'd in form and every limb,
That was on Bolton soon to burst
With rage and hate like, fiends accurst!
Soon glowed the fire warm and bright,
And round him glowed its ruddy light;
And thus he spake, in accents mild,
As might some gentle maid or child:

XXIV.

" Bolton, how did you fare to-day?
Could you not bring the maid away;
Or have you safely brought her here?
If so, where is she? tell me where?
And I will show you how I woo,
And win a lovely maiden, too!
You can lay by this blazing log
And smoke your pipe and drink your grog,
And view the spryest scene, I trow,
You've seen in all your life, till now!
I ll bring a smile upon your brow,
By all the saints on earth, I vow!
Just show to me this lovely bird!
You need not say another word
After you the introduction give,
Is just as true as here I live!

Just pass her out, my jolly boy,
And I will make you mirth and joy!"

XXV.

" Ah, Boss!" old Bolton said, "all day
I did near Logan's mansion stay
Where I could everything survey,
But found no chance to bring away
The precious jewel that I sought;
Only one sight of her I caught;
Upon her porch, the while, she stood,
And so was wrapp'd in cloak and hood
I scarce could see her face at all,
But knew her by her stature tall,
For I was scarce from her a rood;
Cheerful she seemed, and spry of mood,
Some old bird near her had its brood
And she to these was casting food,
Singing a mournful song, the time,
'Bout birds starved midst blast and rime.
Unseen of her I nearer trod,
Till 'tween us scarcely lay a rod;
For all so light I trod the sleet,
And moved from bush to bush sofleet,
She did not hear my padded feet,
Nor yet a sight of me did greet;
But all so hard pour'd down the hail,
And all so piercing drove the gale,
And made such roar and constant sound
Amongst the evergreens around
That densely so the garden crown'd,
And all completely hid the ground.
No other object could be seen
From where she stood amidst the green,

However scant the space between;
Little she thought, the while, I ween,
That anything like human form
Was lurking there midst such a storm.
And just was I upon that maid
In act to make a sudden raid—
Drag her midst the foliage dense,
Bind and gag her, straight bring her hence,
When close at hand I heard a sound
Like coming horse hoofs on the ground;
Plain and more plainer still, mine ear
The clatter of those hoofs could hear,
And soon from where I stood, I spied
Five horsemen to the mansion ride;
Right to the porch they all drew near,
The first was Logan, that I'll swear,
One was Judge Down, that well I know,
I knew him by his locks of snow;
It was his form, from head to feet,
And had his tone of voice complete;
It was Judge Down, I do believe,
Nor think mine eyes could me deceive;
The rest I could not guess at all,
But one among them was so tall,
And showed such comeliness of form,
I fancied he was Crawford Storm;
And so his voice with yours did chime,
It made me marvel at the time
To think what you were doing there
Whom I thought far away elsewhere.

XXVI.

Those five soon in the mansion drew,
And since of them I've had no view,

Not one of them, nor has the maid
Again herself to me displayed;
Though round that house all day I strayed,
Just where I everything surveyed;
And there near froze, midst storm I stood,
And sad to say, for little good,
Till day declined, and night's dark hood
All nature donn'd; with sable snood
Bound tresses of her waving wood,
And draped her boundless form with speed
In her sad, sablest mourning weed.
Then from my hiding place I drew,
Keeping that mansion in my view;
Three times I round its structure pass'd,
My gaze on every window cast,
But not one utter sight I caught
Of the fair maiden that was sought.
Then I to Logan's stable drew,
A saddle on a courser threw,
His halter doff'd, a bridle donn'd,
More swift than ever oath I conn'd,
Right soon on him my form I threw
And from the gloomy stable flew;
But ere I halfway homeward sped
'The worthless courser fell down dead!
Now o'er his loss I shall not weep,
Since fate gave him to me so cheap,
For had he lived I'd kept him here,
Bestowed on him too much of care,
And oft at night I'd lost my sleep
In stealing fodder for his keep.
Logan when dawns to-morrow's morn
Will learn he of a steed is shorn;
But he will never know, I guess,
I made his list of horses less.

Now, Boss, because to-day I failed,
Let not your hope be e'er assailed
With slightest shadow of a fear
Or doubt I ne'er will bring her here;
Give me another day, or two,
And you will have her here to woo;
For nothing can old Bolton daunt!"

XXVII.

" You shall have all the time you want,"
The other with a smile replied,
As he the while old Bolton eyed,
And saw how well the villain lied,
Saw how he strove from him to hide
The fatal failure of that day
That hope was wrecked and cast away!
And never, now, alive or dead,
Would Mary Logan's foosteps tread
Beside them in that dismal bield,
Fate ne'er to them such sight would yield!
And fate from them that maid would shield,
And never give to them a field
For any action 'gainst her more,
On Time's or Eternity's shore!
And all their craft, wile, fraud and force,
Would swerve not fate from such a course.
Well Crawford knew when came the morn
Bolton would from that hut be torn
And beaten to a shapeless mass,
Or else away his life would pass
On foremost tree or gallows grim—
No time or trial spent o'er him;
That frantic men by Ragan led,
Or with John Logan at their head,

Would come in terrible array
And tear him from the hut away;
And all they therein found with him,
Would meet a fate most dread and grim :
Nor would they waste a moment's time
To prove or fix on them a crime;
But other thoughts his spirit swayed—
Him, him, old Bolton had betrayed !
Had lied most grossly, base and vile,
Had treated him with fraud and wile ;
Had traitor been to him through all ;
His treachery had wrought his fall ;
For had he done as he had plann'd,
All things that night would different stand :
Mary had been at his command,
A trembling victim in his hand ;
And Ragan had in dungeon gloom
Sat waiting for his coming doom.
Dread fate his schemes and plans had
        cross'd,
And them in wild confusion toss'd ;
Flowers of hope he'd proudly rear'd,
All, all, had perished, disappeared !
All pass'd away, forever lost,
Cut down by fate's untimely frost,
Ne'er to grow again from out that rime,
Through all eternity or time !
Fate ne'er again the chance would show
For him to deal the slightest blow,
Or any way cause overthrow
To those he loved or hated so.
For he himself that very night,
Must from that country take his flight ;
Must speed to some far distant shore,
Where they will hear of him no more,

Or he'll be cast in dungeon gloom,
Or else the gallows is his doom!
And this all caused by Bolton's guile,
Whom he had trusted all the while;
The traitor! he had caused it all!
Yea, to the dust made Crawford fall;
Heaped on him shame and all things vile,
And for his treachery and wile
Bolton must die a death most grim;
His eye shall glare, his brain shall swim,
With agony in every limb!
And he must feel those pangs through him,
For it is ordered so by fate,
By vengeance, rage, lost hope and hate!

XXVIII.

Though thoughts like these fill Crawford's
      soul,
As burning lava through it roll,
And there tremendous warfare wage,
He secret kept his hate and rage;
His smiling features all belied,
Did workings in his spirit hide;
That seethed like a volcano's core,
Whose outward form and summit hoar,
The snow and sunshine cover o'er;
But soon will burst with fatal roar;
And mild as ever zephyrs blew,
Which not from leaf can shake the dew,
Or on the lake a ripple wake,
He smiling thus to Bolton spake:

XXIX.

" You shall have all the time you want,
Your failure me doth nothing daunt;

I know, old boy, you'll soon succeed,
And when you do, you'll have your meed ;
So just take all the time you need,
And rightly do for me this deed ;
This world did not within a day,
Grow to the thing we now survey ;
It took long days and years of time
To form its plains and hills sublime,
And make its mighty floods that roll,
And stir it like a living soul.
And no great task was ever wrought,
Nor unto great perfection brought,
With wonders all sublimely fraught
Except through patience, time and thought.
Had Homer's soul and mind not caught
This truth, and labor'd as they ought,
This day his story had been naught !
Had ne'er to countless ages taught
How heroes warr'd, how heroes fought—
Against Old Illium,s warriors haught !
How heroes' lives their glory bought,
While they proud Troy's destruction
        sought !
Long years must pass ere trees can grow
Unto the mighty boles they show ;
And time it takes for everything
Nature does to perfection bring.
Time, nature needs to breed a storm,
As well as smaller insect form !
And you'll have all the time you need,
To do for me this little deed.
But when this task you have perform'd,
Your spirit shall with joy be warm'd
Beyond all you can dream of now,
I swear by all on nature's brow.

XXX.

You said you did not use my steed,
But of one Logan's stables freed!
Now I indeed am glad of this,
To-night I would him sorely miss,
If of his life he had been shorn,
For I must reach the town ere morn. "
" O, do not leave us, boss, to-night!
Abide you here till morning's light!
Your steed is safe within my stall,
No harm will unto him befall;
I gave him lots of hay and corn,
Enough to last him unto morn."
" Yes, Bolton, I must go to-night,
And reach the town ere morning's light,
There is a deed I must perform
Ere morn, in spite of night and storm;
I will be back in a day or two,
To see how you the maid pursue."
" Then, Boss, if you will go, just take
A little grog for friendship's sake;
The night is dark, the way is long,
The sleet is cold, the tempest strong,
A little grog will do no wrong;
'Twill fill you full of mirth and song,
And will all through from head to heel,
Make you far better think and feel,
As to the town you journey forth,
Facing cold breezes from the north."
"No, Bolton, no, I scarcely drink,
Ere into drowsy sleep I sink;
So offer me no grog, to-night,
For I must keep my senses bright;

Or I'll not find the road aright
Which leads the shortest way to town,
I o'er some cliff may stumble down,
Or get lost within some wild morass,
You know by such I have to pass.
But ere I go you all I'll treat,
With best of drink you e'er did greet ;
I have with me a flask of wine
From Italy's most choicest vine ;
Since from the grape it came till now,
Full fifteen years have past, I trow ;
In Judge Down's cellar it hath been
Some ten years mellowing, it's seen ;
This morn my uncle's vaults I sought,
This from his favorite barrel brought :
You never drank such wine before,
Next time I come I'll bring you more ;
Now hand three cups, my boy to me,
I'll share it mongst you equally."

XXXI.

Just soon as this had Crawford said,
Forth for some vessel each man sped ;
Three rusty tin cups swift they caught,
And these with haste to Crawford brought.
" Now, Boss," said Bolton eagerly,
I am the oldest of us three,
So, sharing it deal me the most,
And I will give a noble toast ! "
Within the cups the wine was pour'd,
All would the spacious flask afford ;
Ruddy as blood the liquid glow'd
As from the flask to cups it flow'd ;
Swift each man raised his rusty cup,
But ere to lips they brought them up

Old Bolton said, " A toast I'll give :
Long years of joy may Crawford live!
And all his proud and noble race,
May they still keep the foremost place
In all this happy country round,
And ne'er in want and need be found ;
And when here next shall Crawford come,
May I be blind and deaf and dumb—
Yes may the furies seize my breath
And bear me through the vale of death,
If here he doth not find the maid—
If more his wishes be delayed !
My heart is bold as is the rock,
And heeds no storm nor lightning shock ;
My grasp is firm, my arm is strong
As is the flood that sweeps along !
Old Bolton has no laws to fear,
He ne'er will any fetters wear ;
Nor e'er in cell of jail resort,
While Judge Down rules within the court ;
So here's long life, my merry boys,
And one fill'd to the brim with joys,
We'll do our work and fear no noise ! "

XXXII.

Down, down, the ruddy wine was toss'd,
In craving maws from sight was lost ;
Loud each man smacked his lips, and
         swore
That such a luscious drink before
It ne'er had been their fates to taste !
And hoped that time the day would haste
Their Boss would bring them plenty
         more !
" That I will ! " Crawford said, " before

To-morrow's set of sun, I will
Give unto each of you your fill;
But I must leave you now, Adieu! adieu!"

XXXIII.

The door he open swiftly threw
And lightly o'er the threshold drew,
Then closed the door upon their view;
Around the shanty swift he past
To where the window stood, and cast
His vision through the narrow pane
Which smut and dust did amply stain,
And mutterd thus, as there he stood:
"They thought my wine most luscious,
        good;
Little they dream'd in it was mix'd
A poison which has often fix'd
In ghastly pain such subtle knaves,
And brought them to untimely graves!
Slow, slow, it works, but sure as fate.
Soon, soon, they'll feel my deadly hate!
Yea, swift its burning throes will swim
Through every cursed form and limb;
And I shall wait me here and see
Each mortal throe of agony!
I'll watch them how they twist and turn,
Just while it at its height doth burn."

XXXIV.

He said no more, for shriek on shriek,
Did soon their agony bespeak;
And groan on groan told of their throe,
Of mortal and increasing woe!
Writhing from side to side they turn'd,
As if midst scorching flames they burn'd;

Rose from the floor, back on it fell,
With scream and curse and groan and yell;
At one another fierce they sprung,
Their arms around each other flung,
And tussled hard with curse and groan,
Till they upon the floor were thrown;
Then terribly they swore and fought,
At one another's throats they caught;
Until grim death put to a close
Their agony, and tomb-like repose
Did unto Crawford's eye reveal
They neither pain nor life could feel!
Then in the hut he swift return'd,
Though fierce with heat each body burn'd:
Each, each was dead, he soon discern'd,
For with his heel each brow he spurn'd!
Grimly distorted was each face,
Swelling and growing black apace;
Their open eye with horrid glare
Put on a fix'd and ghastly stare;
A gory foam their mouths o'erspread,
From whence yet oozed the bubbles red;
Distorted was each form and limb,
Revealing all the tortures grim
With which their lives had past away,
And swept through them like burning
        spray;
Their rigid arms distended were,
As though they reached for something
        there;
Their fingers all together clinched
As tight as ever vice was pinched;
Their feet were towards their bodies
        brought,
And all in grim distortions wrought;

And seem'd those men from heel to head
So ghastly, horrible, and dread,
Distorted so in form and limb,
Their features racked with writhings grim,
'Twas plain to see some poison dread
Those wretches of their lives had shed.

XXXV.

" Aha! " said Crawford, as he spurn'd
Old Bolton's brow, and roughly turn'd
Each dead man round so he could trace
The swollen features of each face,
" You little dream'd that draught of wine
Did death and hell in it combine !
You'll traitor play to me no more,
Your days for lying now are o'er ;
When morning comes you'll not disclose
The trust I did in you repose ;
Nor to Logan and Ragan tell
My secrets, which you knew too well ;
When here in search of you they come,
They shall find my betrayer dumb.
But had you lived till morning's shine
You straight had ruined me and mine,
For so you saved your cursed neck,
For me or mine you would not reck ;
For this with death I did you strike !
This place must look more business-like
When they come here at morn to search.
So each of you on chairs I perch
Before your limbs too rigid grow ;
You all must make a better show !
You'll all sit up, though dead and dumb,
When here your overthrowers come."

XXXVI.

Three chairs he round the table drew,
In each a lifeless form he threw ;
After much toil, with all his strength
He straightened out their legs full length.
And on the table placed their feet
So each leaned back within his seat ;
Then packs of cards, all soiled, defaced.
Around in each man's lap he placed ;
These were all nicely cut and mix'd.
Then in each mouth a pipe he fix'd ;
And on low stools by every man
Some grog he placed in spacious can.
And said, " When morning comes, I trow,
You all will look as spry as now ;
And should old Logan come at morn,
He will not treat you then with scorn ;
I trow you'll entertain him much,
When he beholds your postures such ! "

XXXVII.

Forth from the shanty Crawford flew.
And down a narrow pathway drew,
And past along a craggy carn
Whose head leaned o'er a sable tarn,
Strode on a narrow path that gave
Scant footway 'tween the rock and wave :
Here soon he gained a wider space
Beneath the rocks, an ample place,
Which through the gloom, appearance
    gave
Of entrance to some spacious cave ;

A match he lit, and gazed around,
There tied secure his steed he found ;
Swift from the place his beast he led
Till he had to the shanty sped,
Then on his back his form he cast,
From out the lonely mountains past,
Till they were far beyond his view,
And towards the town he swiftly drew,
Muttering as he onward hied,
" I really thought old Bolton lied,
I did not think to find at all
My horse within that dismal stall;
Now fly, my steed, my hate and wrath
They'll feel who dare to bar thy path."

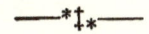

PART VI.

I.

A moment Crawford slacked his speed,
A moment breathed his panting steed,
Which for a halt stood sore in need; ·
And swift himself from saddle freed,
As at the very spot he drew
Where last he did Down's mansion view.
The stately building grand and fair,
No longer met his vision there—
Had like a phantom pass'd away,
There only wreck and ruin lay;
Gone was the stately building all,
The walls that rose so grand and tall,
The lofty cupola and roof,
That seem'd 'gainst time and tempest proof.
The marble steps, the spacious door,
And stately windows, were no more;
All, all, was leveled to the ground,
In darkened heaps of rubbish round;
What had the place with beauty crown'd,
In promiscuous ruin frown'd.
Crawford, bewildered and amazed,
Upon the charr'd, black ruin gazed;
A column tall of sable smoke,
From out the devastation broke;
And from the ruin's centre came
At times huge waves of ruddy flame;
In spite of melting sleet, that fast
The clouds upon the ruin cast,

The embers burn'd with ruddy glow,
Amidst the ruin deep below,
Where in the cellar, wood and stone
Were all in wild confusion thrown.
" What cursed hand this deed has wrought,
Such loss upon my uncle brought ? "
He muttered with bewildered thought,
And mind with grim forebodings fraught.
" Something with Down has gone amiss ;
I straight must learn the cause of this !
Can it be true he's lost his sway,
And all his power past away ?
Has some fell villain done this deed
Through hate, or for some foeman's meed,
Who wished to see the country freed
Of him they always had to heed,
No matter how against their will
Orders he bade them to fulfill ?
No. no. this cannot be at all.
The Judge himself has wrought this fall !
Methinks I now see all things plain,
The wine cup must have drenched his
        brain,
And while he drunk has been, I ween,
He's done as I have often seen
Him do when such has been his mood,
Perhaps to give his fire food,
And just to save himself some toil,
Instead of coal a can of oil
He's on the glowing embers thrown
And all his house to ruin blown,
Himself to atoms torn. but this
I'll shortly learn, know what's amiss."

II.

Thus Crawford thought, then spurr'd his
    steed
And galloped forth with headlong speed.
Soon gained the sleety, winding road
Which led to Wallace's abode;
Then he swift himself of saddle freed.
And in the stable placed his steed;
Right soon he reached that tavern's door.
Right soon he pass'd the threshold o'er:
Around upon that barroom's floor
Lay drunk, the crew of Hugh Lenore;
And there he 'neath the table viewed
The Judge with drink and sleep subdued;
Supine upon the floor he lay,
As senseless as a lump of clay;
And close beside him, Hugh Lenore
Did in a drunken stupor snore;
Behind the bar a taper glowed,
And there the landlord plainly showed;
Like all the rest he senseless lay—
And snored the fleeting time away.
But scarce had Crawford gazed around
On the scene of drunkenness profound,
Than lightly in the room o'erhead,
He thought he heard a footstep tread;
He listened long the truth to prove.
When low again he heard it move:
Then swiftly up the winding stair
He sped, but light as noonday air;
Along a narrow hallway past
And reached a spacious door at last;
That massive door with bolt and bar
Did Crawford's further progress mar;

But through the keyhole Crawford gazed,
A lamp upon the table blazed,
And mighty piles of shining gold
He did beside that lamp behold;
Huge trayes and urns of silverware
He saw beneath that lamplight glare,
And all the mighty ill-got hoard
That landlord there for years had stored.
All thieves to him their plunder brought,
And with his grog their spoil he bought;
Well known was he to every thief,
In fact he was of thieves the chief.
And o'er this board of bright array
With sack in hand, stood Sheriff Fay,
And in it swift the hoard he threw
Till all was out of Crawford's view;
Then on his shoulders strong and broad,
He threw that sack of shining hoard;
But ere unto the door he drew,
Back to the barroom Crawford flew;
From thence unto the street he past
And hid amidst the darkness vast.
But scarcely there had Crawford sped,
Than plain he heard the Sheriff's tread;
Soon saw him ope that tavern's door
And swiftly pass the threshold o'er.
Close it again as swift as light,
And with his sack pass out of sight.

III.

" Curse him ! why did I let him go,
No hindrance to his passage throw?
On earth I have no deeper foe!
I should have laid the villain low;

I should the wily wretch have slain,
And all his sack of treasure ta'en!
How easy, as he closed that door,
Could this right hand have shed his gore!
I could have brained him with a blow,
And he'd never known who laid him low!
Yes, all that hoard I might have ta'en,
And my worst foe on earth have slain—
Left him no more to cross my path,
And make me crouch beneath his wrath!
Curse on this form that idle stood
When offered fate a chance so good!
Curse on this hand that trembled so,
And failed to strike its mortal foe!
Curse on these nerves and fibres all,
For letting fear their action thrall!
And doubly curse my coward soul,
For letting terror it control!
It should have urged this arm amain
Till it yon deadly foe had slain!
Another chance like that, I ween,
Will never more by me be seen!
For well I see this very night,
I from these scenes must take my flight;
Must to some far-of regions go
Where no one Crawford Storm shall
        know;
If here another day I dwell,
They'll lodge me in some dungeon cell
Where I shall waste my life in gloom,
Or else the gallows is my doom;
For in this land my uncle's sway
I plainly see has pass'd away;
Another day, and he will too,
His countless crimes in dungeon rue:

Or else he'll on the scaffold tread,
For many are his crimes, and dread.
That wily Wallace, Hugh Lenore,
And all that round my uncle snore,
Would swiftly noise his crimes abroad
And give him to the hangman's cord,
If slightest chance they saw to save
Themselves from jail, or felon's grave.
You sheriff has senselss drank them all,
So he could surer work their fall;
He will be back ere morning's ray,
And all of them to jail convey.
With Ragan he must be in league,
The two are working some intrigue,
Else Ragan had not ta'en his flight,
From out those prison walls last night.
The Sheriff has the Judge betrayed'
And 'gainst him all his foes arrayed.
Yes, yes, tomorrow's rise of sun,
Will see my uncle all undone—
A captive unto prison led,
His sway and rule forever fled!
But I to him will mercy show—
Will save him from his ruthless foe!
And mine own hand shall deal the blow
That brings his final overthrow;
To-night this tavern I will burn,
And him with it to cinders turn!
Leave here a scene of such array,
'Twill hold his sternest foe at bay!"
This said, he ope'd that tavern's door,
And Crawford strode the threshold o'er;
As closed that door, fierce Crawford's ear
The village clock strike three, could hear.

IV.

Ten minutes past, o'er all that floor
Huge jars of rum did Crawford pour,
And all the whiskey he could see,
He poured around that barroom free
This done, to it a flame he plied,
Which swept o'er all that barroom wide;
Soon from that flame a stifling air
Reigned in that barroom everywhere;
From it was Crawford forced to fly,
Or midst the stifling gasses die;
All through that tavern swift he fled,
And through it flaming fire he spread,
Till all around that inn became
Enveloped in a roaring flame;
Till Crawford saw no chance remained
For it to be by man restrained.
From room to room the fire spread
In one broad torrent vast and red;
The roof, in spite of rain and sleet,
Was wrapp'd in one broad ruddy sheet;
From the windows, above, below,
Out rushed the flame with crimson glow,
Did all that tavern overflow,
Till scarce a spot that inn could show
O'er all its tall and ample frame,
That was not red with scorching flame!
Down, down, the roof with thunder fell,
Into a yawning, raging hell!
Then thousand sparks arose on high
Did on the barn and stable fly;
And joyous welcome found they there—
Shot up in one broad crimson glare;

And every building Wallace owned
Beneath the fiery torrent groaned;
Though rain and sleet was falling fast,
~Furious swept the driving blast,
And fann'd the roaring floods of flame
Till like roaring billows they became,
That in floodtime through the valley roar
And carry all their path before.
Around upon the gloom of night,
Those buildings cast a ruddy light;
From earth to sky their glow they shed,
And o'er the heavens cast their red;
Though walls and roofs went crashing
        down,
Yet no one in the distant town
Heard those smouldering ruins fall,
Nor saw the flames that swallowed all;
So if one of those lost wretches there
Awoke to feel the scorching glare.
He awoke, alas! when all too late
To shun or 'scape his awful fate!
For every door was locked and barr'd,
All chance for flight had Crawford marr'd!
If they awoke 'twas but to die
Midst scorching flames they could not fly.
And thus died three and twenty men,
As vile as e'er trod robber's den;
As e'er felt pangs of love or hate,
Past to a grim, untimely fate;
A horrid end, and by the hand
Of one of their own ruthless band.

V.

With panting steed and rowels red,
Far, far from there had Crawford sped—

For scarce did he the fire start
Ere he did from the scene depart;
Spurr'd on his weary steed until
Some five miles off he gained a hill
That was with scrubby pine o'ergrown,
And little save to outlaws known;
Here Crawford stayed his panting steed,
For rest that horse stood sore in need.
Delighted, on the reddened sky
Did Crawford cast his sable eye;
Enraptured viewed the ruddy glow
Those flames did o'er the heavens throw!
Long space he gazed, his face the while
Was wrapp'd in one unclouded smile;
And as he viewed the distant glow
Thus to himself he muttered low:
" Oh, how my spirit would delight
To stand by yonder scene to-night,
And see each cursed roof and wall
Come tumbling down in headlong fall!
And to have seen the roaring flame,
As it around yon building came!
What glorious scenes they must have made
When they were all in flame arrayed;
And ten years of life I'd freely give
Had I but only twelve to live,
If there to-night I dare have stayed,
And yonder burning men surveyed!
I can't believe those wretches felt
The flames that did their bodies melt!
Ere on the floor the rum was thrown
I sulphur o'er the floor had strown,
A jar of it to flour ground
Placed right behind the bar I found;

Ants, roaches, all vermin grown,
For many years that inn had known,
So Wallace sulphur much employed,
That might this vermin be destroyed.
It was this that made the flame so blue
And gave to all such ghastly hue,
And all so stifling made the air,
Those spreading flames engendered there;
All, all of them were void of breath
And sleeping in the arms of death
Ere the all-devouring flame
Around their senseless bodies came.
Far better they should die this way
Than for their lives in dungeon stay,
With fetters on each manly limb,
Or die upon the gallows grim;
For one of these had been their goal,
Just sure as billows swell and roll;
Yes, yes, just sure as glow is thrown
O'er yonder sky that's not its own.
Little those wretches deem'd, I trow,
Their graves should be so bright as now,
That light for them should thus be given
To guide their fleeting souls to heaven!
Far better thus to take their flight
Than from out dungeon black as night,
Or while the hangman's sable hood
Shuts from the eyesight all things good.
I too, must die, but not like those
Poor fools that in yon flames repose,
Whose brightest joys or wildest woes
Were worth no thought from friends or
    foes;
And ere a score of years have flown
They'll be forgotten and unknown;

Yes, leave no faintest trace behind
To tell there lived such human kind
Back in so short a space of time.
Though they were born and reared in crime,
But common, petty thieves were they,
Who stole by night and slept by day—
Who robbed from those that fate had blest
With wealth they ne'er should have pos-
    sess'd ;
Fools like themselves, who only knew
To grasp what fortune round them threw,
And idly it in bureaus hoard,
Instead of spreading it abroad
For general good of all mankind,
As generous fate had it designed ;
Through joy or woe, through toil and care,
They hoard it for some worthless heir,
Who grieves not, but with joy is wild
When graveyard mold is o'er them piled ;
And scatters soon their years of gain
As clouds cast o'er the earth their rain
Which ne'er to clouds will rise again
But through the earth forever drain.
When all the hoard they heired is down
And they'd to abject paupers grown,
Too lazy and too proud to toil,
They seek their neighbors' hidden spoil,
Reck not how o'er its loss he grieves,
And styles them ruthless, cursed thieves.
Poor pads, they never rise above
A foeman's hate or comrade's love ;
They plod along with that dull throng
Who hardly know the right from wrong,
Who at the best are little things
Frail as the dust on insects' wings,

That gives 'neath light a gaudy glow,
But slightest breath away can blow;
They never seem to dream at all
There is a peak of crime so tall
That those that to its summit go
Can king-like look on those below,
And all unshaken stand above
The realm of passion, hate or love,
But tower there in deathless prime
Beyond the wreck of storm and time,
And leave a record there sublime
Above all men in guilt and crime;
Naught, naught, can dim his dread renown,
Nor bring him from that mountain's crown;
Below he sees the tempest frown,
But lightnings smite it deeper down.
And it shall be my choicest bliss
To mount on that dread precipice
The highest peak of guilt and crime,
And dwell there through all coming time!
Mankind shall shudder at my name
As if a spasm shook their frame,
A horror round my name they'll wreathe,
And fear the very air I breathe;
The maid shall start from out her dream
And waken with a frightful scream.
While terror shakes her soul and form,
And tell she dreamt that Crawford Storm
Had strewn her home with murder dread,
And turned it into embers red!
Mothers shall hush their infants' cry
By telling them that Crawford's nigh,
And neath the quilts they'll hide their
    head
And lie as silent as the dead! ·

And when they hear the winds without,
They'll fancy that they heard me shout;
When fierce at night the tempest moans,
Young men and old, and hoary crones,
Shall all turn pale and quake with fear
And fancy Crawford Storm is near!
In shriek of blast my voice they'll hear,
And tremble lest I shall appear;
Whene'er a barn or mansion's burn'd
Their thoughts will be on Crawford turn'd :
But sound my name, the nun will quail
And on the altersteps turn pale,
Let fall her beads, forget her prayer,
And tremble all with mortal fear!
Yes, at the whisper of my name
She'll quail with thoughts of guilt and
    shame.
Remember all my deeds and crimes
And cross herself a thousand times;
And priests shall shake with mortal fears
When sounds my name upon their ears;
They'll drop their candle, book and bell,
And shake with fears no prayers can quell!
And through long ages this shall last,
E'en when among the dead I've past;
E'en when I'm dead and past away,
My name when breathed shall bring dis-
    may,
As though I walked abroad in life
Scattering death and ruin rife!
Those yet unborn shall dread my name,
And kings shall tremble at the same.
And when my earthly race is run,
'Twill close like set of tropic sun

On a fiery summer day,
When not a cloud obscures his ray;
And not a cloud doth meet the eye
O'er all the regions of the sky,
When all his orb is turned to flame
As red as e'er from furnace came,
And 'neath the hills he drops from sight
And instant leaves the world to night,
No trace of twilight leaves behind.
Doth all the world in darkness bind—
Sends o'er the sky no parting glow,
But takes it all with him below.

VI.

This land I'll fly a little while,
But soon return with beaming smile,
And when old faces I shall meet.
With seeming gladness them I'll greet,
The gentlest manners I will show
To friend, to kinsman and to foe—
I'll be a seeming friend to all,
So I may surer work their fall;
E'en to old Logan I will tell
Within what place his son doth dwell,
Yea, let him know his child doth live,
And rapture to his heart I'll give;
For since the night he lost his child
A grief has o'er his soul been piled
Beneath whose weight of mortal woe
No joy on earth could ease bestow!
And when the joyous news spreads round,
Through Crawford Storm his son was
  found,
Perhaps his rosy daughter's ear
Will deign my words of love to hear,

Although they may seem strange and wild
To one who is so very mild.
Her in my snare I'll soon decoy,
This done, away I'll cast the toy
For Ragan, or some other fool,
To worship till their love shall cool.
Yes, yes, I'll win her love, her trust,
And then I'll cast her to the dust!

VII.

There's only one, now, breathes the air
In all this country far and near,
Who could aught of guilt against me
    swear
And make a crime 'gainst me appear,
And that's the wife of Hugh Lenore,
All, all the rest are now no more;
This very night I've stopp'd their breath
And past them to the vale of death.
If she were dead, I here might stay,
And fear no foe by night or day;
If her from out my way I'd move,
None else could aught against me prove;
No, no! one mortal yet remains
With life still coursing through his veins.
Who knows too much of me, but he
Will never breathe a thing 'gainst me:
I am his confidant and friend,
And ne'er through him my life will end;
The sun from out the sky shall fade,
Ere by his tongue I am betrayed!
And ere he to me traitor prove,
His being from this world I'd move;
And leave my passage clear and free,
Lest he should wrathy wax with me!

Most all my crimes I've done so well,
Who did them, none but I can tell.
But here awhile I will not bide,
Though should it weal to me betide;
Beyond these hills a city stands,
Some forty leagues in foreign lands,
And thither now shall Crawford go,
Betide me weal, betide me woe!
So come, wake up, my gallant horse,
Lend me a while thy noblest force!
If no mischance to us befall,
I soon within some friendly stall
Will lodge thee well, and drink and food
Shall then refresh thy weary mood."

VIII.

Forward that dark bay courser flew,
As if his master's words he knew,
In spite of storm and driving sleet,
Forward he sped as whirlwind fleet;
O'er hill and dale, o'er stream and plain,
Onward he sped with flying mane;
Onward he sped, league after league,
Nor showed that steed the least fatigue:
His massive form and limbs of length
Were built for fleetness, toil and strength,
Each perfect thew and limb was fraught
With all the lightning speed of thought;
Deep his shoulders, broad his breast
As ever yet a steed possessed;
His arching neck and comely head
Showed him from best of chargers bred.
His nostrils wide and flashing eye
Showed him of mettle proud and high;

A nobler formed and stronger horse
Ne er stemm'd a storm nor torrent's force.

IX.

Fleet as the wind or mountain roe,
O'er pathless wilds did Crawford go;
And many leagues had Crawford fled
Ere night before the morning sped;
Rose round him forests broad and vast,
But these on tempest's wings he past;
Broad, open fields before him lay,
O'er these like thought he made his way,
Until a ridge of hills he gained
Where all in barren grandeur reigned
Around, about on every hand
Tall rocks rose up sublime and grand,
While here and there a scrubby pine
Leaned o'er each granite's steep incline;
Between tall lines of winding rocks
That seem'd riven by earthquake shocks,
So craggy, disolate and wild
They were upon each other piled,
Which left a rough and narrow road;
His bounding steed did Crawford goad;
Cold blew the wind, the hail and sleet
Hard on the steed and rider beat;
But on, in spite of cold and blast
Along that rugged road they past:
That narrow pass so wild and strange
Throughout whose drear and dismal range
Were pits and fearful chasms found
That sunk far in the rocky ground,
And did no sign of bottom show
To longest lines e'er cast below,
Down which did roaring torrents flow;

When the sunshine's radiant glow
To liquid turned the ice and snow
That winter o'er those hills did throw;
And when the rain in summer time
Came pouring o'er that rocky clime,
And swell'd to torrents deep and strong
And dashed that rocky pass along,
Down through these chasms dead and deep
Away from sight the floods would sweep,
Rush in one tumultuous mass,
From sight within the chasms pass:
And none within that country round
Perhaps, save Crawford could be found,
Along that fearful pass would ride
For all the gold that country wide!
Strange tales about that pass were told
That awed the boldest of the bold;
With glowing eyes and lips apart,
With trembling form and throbbing heart,
Would listening peasants sit to hear
Its tales of wonder and of fear!
How at a certain time of night
An all-unearthly, hellish light
Would from each horrid pit emerge
While spectres danced around its verge;
And from them horrid monsters came
With eyes of fire and tongues of flame,
With mouths that stream'd forth clotted
    gore,   *
With hands that murdered mortals tore:
And awful forms, terrific, strange,
Along that fearful pass would range!
On high would gory daggers gleam,
And oft would come unearthly scream;

Huge, fleshless forms and goblins grim
Of monstrous shape and horrid limb,
The peasants swore they'd seen at night
From out those chasms take their flight;
For ages had those tales been told
About this pass, and young and old
Believed them true, yea, all around
Believed that pass was haunted ground!
And all that round that region dwelt
For that wild pass a horror felt;
And not one breathing mortal there
At night would to that pass repair,
And view its dreadful scenes alone
For all the gold to mortals known!
Not e'en alone on brightest day
Through it would any peasant stray;
Right seldom was that rocky glen
E'er trod by foot of mortal men.
" The Devil's Rift," this pass was called,
In prose and tales of rhyming Scald;
It had been known by that sole name
Since first to sight of man it came.

X.

Though well did daring Crawford ken
The peasant's tales about this glen,
For these he no more thought nor cared
Than for a leaf that's torn and scared;
Yea, he thought of them no more the while
Than for an infant's frown or smile.
Right well each pit and chasm grim
Within that pass was known to him;
He oft by them had ta'en his way,
By darkest night and brightest day;

Knew just where every chasm yawned
As well as when the morning dawned.
And could by each his charger rein
As safe as o'er a level plain;
Along that rocky pass full well he knew
No other traveler's footsteps drew,
And him no mortal man would view
To tell upon what course he flew ·
If Logan chanced to take the whim
Upon that morn to search for him ;
Beside, three leagues he gained, and more,
In journeying those mountains o'er,
And traveling to the town he fled,
Taking that road so lone and dread ;
Around those hills fair was the way,
But it was travelled night and day,
And Crawford wished no human eye
His journey on that morn to spy,
For this through short-cuts lone and dread,
From travelled ways had Crawford fled.

XI.

With tightened rein and rowels red
Throughout The Devil's Rift he sped.
And here a beaten road he found
Which round that range of mountains
    wound ;
Beyond far as his eye could view.
Were forests dense as ever grew,
Huge oak and pine and giant elm.
And gum and poplar, clad the realm;
A rolling country decked with wood
All, all, beyond those mountains stood,
And no abode of human kind
Amidst its range the eye could find.

XII.

" My gallant steed, from sleet and storm
I soon will lodge thy weary form!
Thy strength that I this night have shorn
I will repair with hay and corn ;
Beyond, where stands yon woody hill,
Flows clear as glass a crystal rill,
And thou of it shall have thy fill,
Let fate betide us good or ill !
It flows beside a lonely inn,
Where we from sleet shall shelter win;
Yes, now let good or ill befall
I'll tarry there, within its stall
An hour's rest I'll give to thee,
E'en Logan there himself I see !
And e'en though while I tarry so,
Ragan and every mortal foe
Should gain upon the path I go!"

XIII.

Thus to his steed he muttered low,
And gained the woody hill, where rose
An inn midst forests clad with snows;
Some giant trees leaned o'er its form,
As though to shield it from the storm;
Aged as those trees, that inn appeared,
And out of craggy rocks was reared ;
Together all its walls were placed
Firm as the hill on which 'twas based ;
All about it save its mossy roof,
Was unto storm and fire proof;
Nor was that inn of humble size,
Majestically did it arise,

Like some grand old feudal tower,
When decay displays its power,
That yet can show through storm and time
Some traces of its ancient prime—
That while it stands, nor years nor storm
Shall deface, nor utterly deform;
But will to every mortal eye
That shall its wasting strength discry.
Long as its stately walls shall last
Convey some glory of its past;
And bid them all in it behold
The wonders of the days of old!
Strange tales about that inn were told,
Of crimes and murders manifold;
And one is told about the race
That last had owned that ancient place:
" Two brothers," so the story runs,
And thus told from sires to sons,
" Together heired that ancient hall,
And boundless tracts of forest tall;
And there high mirth those brothers held.
As ever mortals did of eld;
The song and dance and joyous feast
Ne'er in that ancient castle ceased;
From night till morn, from morn till night,
All in that place was wild delight!
For young and old, that country round,
Glad welcome in that castle found.
Yea, there did youths and maidens throng
And join the feast and dance and song;
The flowing ale or wine-cup quaff'd,
Away with mirth the fleeting hours laugh'd.
But on one night, while round the board
The mirth, the jest, and revel roared,

And ruddy wine in goblets glowed
Pure as e'er yet from vineyards flowed,
And all seem'd round as void of woe
As any scene all earth could show,
As free of every worldly care
As ever yet did mortal share,
There came a strange and dismal sound,
As though an earthquake shook the
        ground;
And o'er the festive board a cloud
Came rushing on with thunders loud;
In air it paused above the heads
Of those two lords, and darkness spreads
So dense throughout that festive place,
No one could see his neighbor's face;
While from that dark and awful cloud,
Thus spake a voice as tempest loud:

XIV.

" Seducers of the young and fair,
Who've brought the pure to grim despair!
Betrayed, forsook, despoiled, deceived
Those who in ye trusted and believed—
The innocent, the pure and good,
Who before ye chaste as angels stood!
Ye've filled their souls with grim despair,
And brought them to an early bier!
Why shall ye longer live to curse
The light of this bright universe?
This very night ye'll meet your doom,
And pass to everlasting gloom!
But ere ye go, your crimes review,
Which wrath Divine upon ye drew!"
Then ceased the voice, so dread and loud,
And lightnings filled the awful cloud!

A panorama all of woe
Flashed midst the cloud's increasing glow.
It moved along in rapid flight,
Revealing many a ghastly sight
Of maids betrayed and left forlorn
Beside their infants newly born,
Who sought to hide their guilt and shame
By either poison, flood or flame!
And as the picture flashed along,
More awful did the coffins throng;
Women with babes of tender frame
In coffin after coffin came,
Till all that scene naught else disclosed
But coffins, where the dead reposed!
Then, last of all, a spectre came
Upon that cloud of flashing flame;
A spectre dread, of horrid mold
As ever yet did hell behold
Amidst all the dread and grimest forms
Its winter chills or summer warms!
Its head was like the dragon grim,
Like anaconda was each limb;
Twas like the crocodile in form,
But black as clouds of thunder storm;
Its eyes were red as coals of flame,
And from them awful lightnings came!
Dread and more dread the spectre grew,
As nearer towards those lords it drew,
And from its mouth that stream'd with
        smoke
An awful voice like thunder broke,
But what it said, no mortal there
Knew one sole sound that reached his ear;
'Twas in the tongue of some strange land
No mortal there could understand!

As spake the spectre fierce and loud,
To utter darkness grew the cloud,
An awful blackness filled the room,
And thunders shook the horrid gloom,
And screams burst forth as dread and 'ghast
As e'er on ears of mortals past!
And with these screams, from out the
  room
Swift as thought sped forth the cloud of
  gloom,
Throughout the spacious windows past,
With all the roar of simoom blast,
Or like the roar of floods long pent,
That through their barriers find vent.
But when that awful cloud had sped,
Each guest looked round with mortal
  dread!
The lights around that banquet glowed,
And clear as day their brightness flowed
On everything within that room,
But over every soul a gloom
And horror dread and grim was cast
As ever yet o'er mortal past,
For nowhere in that hall around
Could those two lords be seen or found!
And never from that awful night
Were they e'er seen by mortal sight!
That horrid spectre, fierce and grim,
Had ta'en those lords away with him!" '
A hundred tales like this were told
About that castle strange and old,
And all the peasants far and near
Had for that place a mortal fear.
And when they neared that haunted hold
Straight grew their blood and marrow cold.

XV.

Soon to that inn fierce Crawford rode
And o'er its stately threshold strode;
A hoarygroom came at his call
And led his charger to the stall.
Right in the barroom Crawford came
Where sat the landlord and his dame;
A very aged pair were they,
With wrinkled brows and tresses gray:
But neither form was bent through time,
Erect they stood as in their prime.
The landlord in his youth had been
A figure of commanding mien;
Tall was his form, his shoulders broad
Did with his brawny breast accord,
His thewy limbs of ample length
Displayed a lion's peerless strength,
His massy arms and spacious hands
Contained the force of iron bands,
And well his brawny neck displayed
The giant thews of which 'twas made.
On which as comely head was placed
As e'er an Anglo Saxon graced;
Did o'er his manly features flow
A heavy beard as white as snow,
Which o'er his brawny bosom rolled
Like ridge of snow on Northern wold,
His mouth, that heavy beard beneath.
Revealed itself with peerless teeth;
These, these, were just as perfect still
As in their prime; but stubborn will
Those thin, pale, curving lips revealed
That neither age nor beard concealed;

They had a stubborn, haughty curve,
Did ne'er from their fix'd purpose swerve,
And in that head an eye was placed
Whose brightness time had not defaced,
Small, bright gray eyes, of twinkling glow.
Shone 'neath shaggy brows the hue of
 • snow,
When just within the cloud 'tis wrought
And not a taint of earth has caught;
And seemed his forehead, high and broad,
To have much knowledge 'neath it stored;
O'er it did hoary tresses rest
White as the foam on ocean's breast,
Or like the mists that bask at night
Beneath the full moon's silver light;
Like prophet of the olden time
He seem'd, and was as free of crime
As any one in human mold
Who ever lived to be so old.
Like him, his aged, hoary dame,
Had been as comely in her frame;
Ne'er a more perfect female form
Felt summer's heat nor winter's storm;
Than hers a foot more light and true
Did ne'er its path through life pursue,
'Twas like the fall of fleecy snow,
Or move of air when zephyrs blow,
Soft as the echoes of a song
Whose dying strains the hills prolong;
Her lips and cheeks all still were fair
As any fann'd by vital air,
And still her ruby mouth revealed
The pearly teeth it half concealed;
Ne'er a more sweet and comely face
Yet smiled amongst the human race,

'Neath arching brows that heavy flowed
Her sable eyes like lightnings glowed,
Flashed like the diamond's starry ray
When full on it the sunbeams play,
And rose her forehead high and broad,
Like that of her own ancient lord.
So seem'd this aged, hoary pair,
That Crawford Storm encountered there.

XVI.

For fifty years had they been wed,
And joy and grief had to them sped ;
Their share of both, this pair had known,
Though of grief the largest share was
    shown,
Yet still they loved as fond and true
As when their morn of life was new ;
Yea, that love had far stronger grown,
As on the stream of years had flown ;
The love that had between them sprung
When they were buoyant, gay and young,
Had been like mortar the mason throws
Between two solid rocks, that grows
Firm as the rocks themselves, through
    time,
Through summer's heat and winter's rime,
Unites those rocks so sure and fast
They all become as one at last ;
Nor will it let them sundered be,
Though floods may dash around it free ;
Nor sundered will it let them go
Unto the sturdy workman's blow ;
The granite rocks themselves may break,
Its hold on them it won't forsake

Although should earthquakes rend the
　　plains.
Thus bound with adamantine chains
Of love, in their old age this couple dwelt.
And all each other's joys and sorrows felt.

XVII.

So wild the tales had rumor told
About that castle gray and old,
All held the place in awe and fear
And seldom ever ventured near;
All peasants in that country round,
Believed the place was haunted ground,
Also believed that hoary pair
Were just the ones for them to fear;
Some swore they'd seen that aged dame
Change water into hissing flame!
Transform a cat till it became
An old man, crippled, blind and lame;
Seen her oft in open day
Mount on a single spear of hay
High up in air o'er forests tall,
And fly around that castle wall;
Seen her o'er broadest torrents leap,
Followed in air by flocks of sheep;
And all believed this aged pair
Held nightly commune dread and drear,
With all those forms so grim and strange
That in The Devil's Rift did range;
All round them held them so in awe,
Their neighbors seldom e'er they saw
But all strangers, and many, too,
Who 'long that noted highway drew,
Held in high esteem that aged pair,
And praised their virtues grand and rare

Abroad their virtues wide were blown,
And as the good old pair were known,
But mongst their nearer neighbors there
They both were shunn'd with mortal fear.
Nine sons and daughters they had seen,
Of sprightly souls and comely mien,
But eight were lying still and low
On yonder hill beneath the snow;
In early life they pass'd away,
To him who fashioned night and day;
One son alone to them remained,
Whose soul they knew with guilt was
    stained;
Was steeped in every loathsome crime
That ever yet was known to time;
Had often them with blows abused,
And every way he could, misused:
And yet they loved him fond and wild
As ever parents loved a child,
Although it was that son who told
To all the peasants young and old,
The tales about that aged pair
Dealing in rites most grim and drear;
Of bringing round them spectres dread,
That did at night that castle tread;
And fill'd with tales each rustic's ear
Till them they shunn'd with mortal fear!
And once had roused the rustics so
That they had plann'd one day to go
And that old haunted place o'erturn,
And that gray pair of witches burn!
And they had felt their wrath and hate—
Most horrible had been their fate,
Had it not chanced upon that day
Some score of travelers passed that way.

Who oft had in the castle stayed
And there their home o'ernight had made.
When they the rustic clowns, beheld
And learned the cause which had impell'd
Those rustic fools to seek the life
Of that old landlord and his wife,
Back the furious throng they fought,
And from their hands the old pair brought,
Forced promise from that rustic throng,
They ne'er would do this old pair wrong.

XVIII.

Yes, all this pain and trouble grew,
And every source of grief they knew,
With which their aged souls were wrung
By one base wretch who'd from them
        sprung,
Who should have been their foremost
        friend,
The first to shelter and defend,
And happy made their closing life
By spreading round them comforts rife,
Instead of everlasting strife.
Would God that he had pass'd away
Where all the rest in silence lay,
Nor left one cursed trace behind
To tell his fate to human kind!
For harder heart and sterner soul
Did never human form control!
Oh, gaze upon that aged pair
As cruel Crawford standeth there,
Such likeness in the three you see,
You'd swear their son must Crawford be:
In him the mother's eyes are seen
That flashed on all with lightning sheen,

Dark were they as the womb of night,
But flashed bright as electric light;
His was the mother's airy tread
And his the mother's comely head,
Like hers, his voice was soft and low,
Sweet as music's sprightliest flow;
But his tall form and swelling chest
Was like that the sire possessed,
With him was that commanding mien
Like ever in his sire was seen.

XIX.

Across the floor tall Crawford drew,
His arms around his mother threw,
And placed upon her aged brow
One kiss as cold and soft as snow,
And with a smile as meek and bland
He grasped his hoary sire's hand.
And while his face serenely smiled,
He thus began with accents mild:
" Not as of old I greet you now,
With saucy tongue and haughty brow:
I come not now with threat and blow,
But in submission, meek and low;
And not a word you now shall hear
That is not welcome to your ear,
For I do regret with all my soul
I ever caused your spirits dole,
And mourn with all my heart and mind
I ever treated you unkind
And served you not like loving son,
For such from me you should have won,
For kind to me you've always been
As any parents ever seen,

And much my spirit doth regret
My actions ever made you fret;
Henceforth, I swear by all that's good,
And let my words be understood,
Never by any deed nor thought,
Though unto me a crown it brought,
Shall aught on earth by me be wrought
Will make your souls with sorrow fraught;
Still kind and true to you I'll be,
As you both have ever been to me!
But mother, mine, I've journeyed long,
The way was rough, the tempest strong,
Some ruddy wine would do no wrong;
With it methinks a little food
Would soon refresh my weary mood,
And make your son far better feel
Through all his form from head to heel."

XX.

The while his aged mother stored
With food and wine the spacious board,
His sire forth a letter drew,
Which unto Crawford's hand he threw.
" Read this, my son," the old man said.
The letter Crawford open spread,
And this unto himself he read:
     Richard Storm :—
               When thou read this o'er
I shall with the living be no more,
So do the little deed for me
That I herein shall crave of thee ;
See all I ask is promptly done.
The bearer is John Logan's son,
Whose abduction years ago I wrought;
I wish him to his father brought,

And knowing thou art Logan's friend,
And by thy inn the boy must wend
To reach the place his father dwells,
For unto me thy Crawford tells
John Logan lives just as of yore
Where I from him his infant bore;
See that the old man finds his boy,
And crown his latter days with joy;
Let rapture dwell in sorrow's stead.
For long he's thought his infant dead.
Now, twenty years have flown, and more,
Since I hired Bolton and Lenore
To crush his life and blast his joy,
By bringing me his rosy boy.
To foreign climes with him I fled,
And in a Convent had him bred;
I hid the infant so secure
His sire ne'er had found him more,
Though he'd trebled all the vast reward
He offered to have his child restored.
But why from him his child I stole,
Shall ne'er be known by living soul!
That secret is but known to me,
And uttered it shall never be;
Down to the grave with me 'twill pass,
And wither with this mortal mass.
But tell John Logan this, for me,
Of other crimes 'gainst him I'm free;
I did not burn his barn, nor tell
My men to do a deed so fell;
'Twas Hugh Lenore's and Bolton's hand
That turned them to a flaming brand:
Why they did is unknown to me,
And I of all that crime am free.

Enough through me this boy shall heir
To all his father's loss repair,
As far as burning barns shall go,
But I cannot repay the woe
His sire all these years has borne,
Since from his sight his child was torn ;
But this I would not, if I could, repay,
Though it brought all earth beneath my
    sway,
Or for that deed this fleeting soul
Should one-half of heaven control !
I've hated Logan all my life,
With loathing ever strong and rife.
And evermore, through good or ill.
My spirit shall detest him still !
I damn him with my latest breath,
And I shall curse him after death !
If e'er in other worlds we meet,
Still he in me a foe shall greet,
Who ne'er forgets and ne'er forgives
Long as his deathless spirit lives !
But here upon my bed of death
I can say with my latest breath,
I ne'er a harm to Logan wrought,
Save that from him his child I brought ;
To injure him by deed or thought
In other way, I've never sought.
The night we stole his child from him
I saved him from a death most grim.
For while he fought the roaring flame
That fast around his building came,
While he yet lingered in a stall
Beneath a burning building tall
Which then was just about to fall,

Old Bolton's hand had closed the door;
From there he ne'er had issued more;
For 'neath the falling ruin vast
Midst smoke and flame he'd breathed his
    last!
But sternly I the deed forbade,
And Logan's life I longer made.
For one I hate I would not kill,
Death frees them of their grief and ill;
Such mercy I could never show
To any one I deem'd my foe;
No, let their life no ending know,
For length of days is length of woe.
A twelvemonth now has nearly flown
Since unto Crawford Storm 'twas known
Where I was with the boy concealed:
To him I all the facts revealed,
And made him promise me, that he
Just soon as I of life was free,
Which well I knew would shortly be,
He'd give John Logan back his son,
And tell him I the theft had done,
And let blame on none but me be laid!
Thy son my confidant I made
For reasons only known to me,
Save what I herein tell to thee,
And with thee let it hidden be:
Some things about thy son I know—
Some crimes he did long, long ago;
If they were only noised abroad
They'd give him to the hangman's cord;
And were those deeds but told to thee,
Thy love for him would blasted be;

Thy hoary hair would stand on end,
And death pangs through thy heart would
        wend ;
Throughout thy veins the crimson blood
Would cease to move, be frozen flood !
I trust him, for he knows too well
While living on this earth I dwell,
His life and fame are in my hands,
By me he either falls or stands !
My tale is done, my race is run ;
See thou that Logan gets his son.
And what I've said to Crawford tell,
Let him explain to Logan well
All facts about my theft and flight,
I made to him all plain as light.
        Farewell !   Yours,   Etheldred."

XXI.

                        A frown
Dark as the cloud on mountain's crown
That rolling thunder smiteth down
Unto the gloomy vale below,
Where deepening shades of darkness grow ;
So dark, so grim, grew Crawford's wrath,
And o'er his visage showed its path.
From off his chair he instant sprung.
The letter on the floor he flung
And on it placed his heel, and said
" Thus will I trample Etheldred !
I'll make the lying wretch deny
What he has said, or he shall die !
No deed of crime he knows 'gainst me
Than I know of the Polar Sea !
Full twenty years, I'll swear, have pass'd
Since I on him have looked my last ·

At least my sight he has not cross'd
Since poor old Logan's child was lost!
His story is all rhyme and jingle,
In which sense and nonsense mingle,
But won't, like wine and water, mix;
No crime on me that wretch can fix
But what I from my name shall move,
And him a doted liar prove!
Enough of him.   Come, mother mine,
Give me some food and rosy wine."

XXII.

Across the floor tall Crawford strode,
Where on the board the red wine glowed;
To the brim he fill'd a spacious cup,
But ere to his lips he brought it up
He thus the aged pair address'd:
" May my soul ne'er know a moment's rest,
Nor reach the kingdom of the blest,
But ever be with woe distress'd
If I don't clear my name and fame
Of all this infamy and shame;
And may this draught of ruddy wine
Ne'er pass within these lips of mine,
If I don't prove old Etheldred
The falsest liar ever bred!
Prove there's no truth in what he's wrote,
More than a crag of rock will float
Like cork upon the water's breast!
Yes, trust your son will never rest
Till he shall crown your days with joy,
And your old age shall bless your boy!

XXIII.

Down went the ruddy wine; again
The cup he filled; once more did drain;
Three times he filled it to the brim,
And three times the cup was drained by
    him.
And never yet a hungry steed
E'er ate a meal with greater greed,
Than Crawford soothed his hungry mood
With ruddy wine and smoking food;
For two full days at least had flown,
Since Crawford drink or food had known.
The while he ate, his father's eye
Did full on Crawford's features lie,
The while he gazed he well could trace
The features of the mother's face—
When she was happy, bright and young,
And with no age nor sorrow wrung!
Yes, like when first she graced his side,
His partner and his gentle bride.
And while he gazed, the old man's soul
Yearned with a love beyond control
For that vile wretch who only sought
To injure those fate round him brought.
Right well the father knew his child
Was all treacherous, base and wild,
And was to him as false and vile
As any villain skill'd in wile;
Yet for that son his spirit thrilled
With love warm as ever bosom filled;
All that son's foul abuse and guile
His heart and soul forgot the while;
Nor did the old man doubt one word
That he from out his Crawford heard;

And all that letter said, he thought
Were lies as foul as e'er were wrought.

XXIV.

With ruddy wine and smoking food
Had Crawford soothed his hungry mood,
Then thus addressed that aged pair
In accents gentle, soft and clear:
" Parents, methinks I heard you say
Young Logan left here yesterday? "
" We did," the father straight replied ;
" I with him sent a trusty guide,
And if they have not travelled slow
And kept the road I bade them go,
Their journey by this time is done,
And Logan has his long lost son.
Thank God, the old man's grief is o'er!
And may he never sorrow more,
I wish him joy with all my soul,
And gladness unalloyed with dole ! "
" If wishing brings the least of good,
And such it does, I've understood,
I wish him all joy in nature wide,"
Crawford with beaming smile replied.
" But if his boy's been reared and bred
By such a fiend as Etheldred,
I'd not much for his morals give ;
I trust no greater scamp doth live!
But then, for this we need not care,
I trust he'll seldom journey here.'
" Nor I," the father swiftly said,
" I never liked old Etheldred,
For in his dark, deceitful eye
Was craft and guile of deepest dye,

I shunn'd him as some adder grim,
Yet, never was unkind to him;
But we are of that villain free,
If Logan has not lied to me;
He said the old man's mind of late,
Grew to a melancholy state,
Each day he seem'd to grow more sad,
Then, like a dog, died raving mad!"
" 'Tis well, indeed, if thus he died,
For the way he on me has lied
In yonder note; when next we met
To punish him I'd not forget.
But a feeling in my breast doth lurk
That tells that mischief is at work;
So straight from here I now must go,
Though falls the sleet and tempests blow:
I'll shortly see who in this land
'Gainst me will dare to lift their hand,
And say I ever did a deed
That unto any crime would lead!
But while I'm gone, if any wretch
The slightest tale to you should fetch
About your son, straight you reply.
You know their tale to be a lie.
And breathe you in no mortal ear
When last your Crawford journeyed here.
And breathe you to no friend nor foe
That I from here this day did go;
I'll thwart the schemes of foemen all,
If any such have plann'd my fall!
But ere I go, give me all hoard
That both your purses can afford;
Sure as on your hearth the embers burn,
Within a week I will return

Each mite you lend to me this day,
And with it ample interest pay."

XXV.

Some thirty coin of shining gold,
All, all, that did their purses hold,
And all the hoard on earth they owned,
They swift unto their Crawford loaned.
" Could you swear that this is all the gold
That is by both of you controlled ?
Have you no stockings stowed away
That would far more of it display,
If you two only chose to bid
Them brought from places where they're
    hid ?
Fear not to lend it all to me,
No mite of it shall squandered be ;
I'll give it not the least abuse,
But put it to a proper use."
" No other mite have we, my son,
As you have bid us, we have done,
And loaned you every mite we own :
Think not that we have misers grown
In our old days, and would not give
All we possess to make you live
Contented both in soul and mind ! "
" Parents, it grieves me sore to find
And thus to see Dame Fortune's hand,
Gave not far more to your command ;
Far more than this, I really thought
You could have from your purses brought
To aid me on the path I go,
And you far more than this could show.
But I must be content with this—
I go—Farewell! May joy and bliss,

Long life on earth and ruddy heal'h,
With ceaseless inflow of vast wealth,
Be my dear aged paren's' lot,
And I by them be ne'er forgot!
Farewell, a little while!"

XXVI.

The door
He open drew, and pass'd the threshold
     o'er,
Which nevermore beheld the form
Nor knew the tread of Crawford Storm.
Soon from the stall his steed was brought
Whose mane within his hand he caught,
And swift as ever greyhound sprung
Upon the deer, or to guard her young,
On foes the leaping panther flew,
His form he in the saddle threw,
And swift as breath of mountain blast,
Adown the hill from sight he pass'd.
Long, long, those aged, hoary twain
Watched him who ne'er returned again;
E'en when from them he disappeared
Midst forests vast before them reared,
Alone they in the doorway stood,
And watched afar that boundless wood,
Though icy blasts upon them blew,
And wild their hoary tresses flew,
Like shreds of ta'tered snow-white sail
That round the masts stream on the gale;
Far other thoughts their hearts controll'd,
Nor did they feel the tempest's cold;
No other thought their spirits knew
Than him who parted from their view;

And after him their feelings flew
Till all else oblivious grew
Save that child's sorrows, weal or woe—
Those souls no other feelings know ;
Nor from the door the old pair drew
Till shades of night around them grew,
And sky and hill and forest vast,
From sight in utter darkness past.
Day after day this old pair stood
And gazed upon that boundless wood,
Which dense o'er earth its shadow spread
And hid the path their child had fled,
But never to their sight he came ;
Nor did despair their spirits tame ;
Grim, gaunt Despair could never cope
With the brawny arm of stalwart Hope!
E'en stronger, far, is Hope, than Death,
And lingers with man's latest breath ;
Bright Hope! with her flaming sword and
        targe,
Comes as a river red and large :
Through serrid ranks of grim Despair,
Hews down her passage broad and clear ;
Through realms of night makes sure her
        way,
And turns them all to brightest day.
And hope each aged soul beguiled ;
They watched the coming of their child
With hope that warmed each bosom's core
As furnace glows with molten ore,
And day by day they wept or smiled,
And watched the coming of their child
Till blind with age those old ones grew,
Yet no sight nor sound of him they knew.

O;t, pathless wood! oh, lonely wild!
Will ye return no more their child?
What ye receive, will ye no more
From out your lonely realm restore?
A wandering roe or startled deer,
A tree fell'd by the storm's career,
Is all from out that forest drear
Those old ones ever see or hear.

XXVII.

'Twere long and useless now, to tell
O'er what mountain, valley, hill and dell
Crawford pass'd, and what to him befell,
As on he rode with all the speed
That lay within his gallant steed,
O'er byways dismal as his thought,
And reached the city that he sought.
By night and day, by day and night,
He paused not in his onward flight,
Though hard it blew and hailed and rained.
Till he the wished-for city gained.
'Twas dead of night when there he drew,
One lamp its light on darkness threw
As up a narrow court he rode,
Which led unto a vast abode;
High through the darkness and the gloom
Did its tall walls and spires loom.
Within, it was as silent all
As was its dark and massive wall
All looked as dark and desolate
As is the outlaw felon's fate,
Who treads alone his dungeon room
The night before he meets his doom,

Who knows when morning lights the sky,
He shall upon the gallows die !
Before a gate as black as night
Did Crawford from his steed alight,
A secret spring he touched, and straight
A tread was heard behind the gate.
A sound within of heavy keys
Unlocking bolts came on the breeze.
Soon the gate was open cast
And through it steed and rider past.
Then swift the gate was closed once more,
And bolted, locked, and barr'd secure.
So dark and dismal was the place,
E'en scarcely Crawford's eye could trace
The features of that mortal's face,
Who there to him admitance gave
Midst silence solemn as the grave.
Too well that silent porter knew
What step beside that gateway drew
Soon as was touched that secret spring.
To ask of him one single thing.
Right oft had Crawford pass'd that gate
On such a night, and just as late ;
E'en dogs within that spacious yard
That nightly there were placed on guard,
Knew well that steed, knew well that man,
And whining welcome, round them ran.

XXVIII.

His steed to stall the porter led,
While o'er that yard tall Crawford sped
And reached a door of that abode
Through whose wide transom lamplight
      glowed ;

Along a winding hall he past
And gained a spacious room at last;
Huge logs of oak and pine were stowed
Upon a hearth that cheerful glowed,
And cast their warmth around the room.
And with their light dispell'd the gloom.
Before those embers' cheerful glow,
There sat a man whose locks of snow
In heavy, wavy, ringlets spread,
Around a manly, comely head;
Hung o'er a forehead broad and high,
'Neath which there shone a piercing eye—
Huge, flashing eyes, so dark and bright
They dazzled each beholder's sight.
Perhaps it was his brows of snow
Which made them seem of such dark glow.
His cheeks were hollow, pale and lean,
And these of hair were shaven clean.
But on his chin a scanty beard
The hue of purest white appeared;
And on his upper lip a vast
Mustache of white was spread, that cast
So long and dense a growth below,
He could of mouth no vestige show;
But 'tween those beardless cheeks arose
An all-abundant mass of nose;
Far out it reached, and downward curved
Towards his mouth like beak of parrot
    swerved;
He was a man whose iron nerve
Did aye his will obedient serve;
As firm of purpose, strong of will,
As rocks that prop the solid hill;
Sooner the sun might change his course,
The swollen stream forget its force

And instant stop its rapid flow
To open gulfs that yawn below,
Than he would swerve from any scheme
His will had plann'd, though it might teem
With dangers all as dread and grim
As e'er brought loss of life and limb;
Some way he'd find his deed to do,
Had he to search all nature through.
Of smile or frown no faintest trace
Was ever seen upon his face;
O'er every thought that stirr'd his soul
His will held absolute control;
Of joy or woe, of pain or fear,
And all the passions mortal heir.
He seem'd as void as is the stone
That dwells midst ice on mountains lone:
A pipe within his mouth he held,
From which were clouds of smoke im-
    pell'd.
Before the warm hearth Crawford drew,
His hat and cloak from off him threw,
Shook off the clots of frozen snow,
Before that fire's ruddy glow
Upon a chair his robe he spread
To dry before those embers red.
Then to the old man thus he spoke,
Whose face was hid midst clouds of smoke:

XXIX.

" I see your mind again is fraught
With some o'erwhelming rush of thought,
Which doth your spirit all o'erflow:
I really don't believe you know
That Crawford's form is standing now
Here right before your beaming brow!

I don't believe my words you hear,
Though breathed so loud upon your ear!
And were not for the smoke I see
Arising from your pipe so free,
I would have sworn that you were dead,
Or to the land of dreams had sped!
But Ryan, is there any word
Of news about our plot you've heard?
If so, wake up and tell me all,
Nor silent gaze on yonder wall,
As some old corpse for hours dead!"
" I was just thinking." Ryan said,
" If rightly should the plot succeed,
How glorious will be our meed!
Soon as the morn the day shall bring
We herald in another king,
We'll be next to him in power,
For we are promised ample dower!"
" Think you he'll make his promise good?
For seldom kings have faithful stood
To any promise, oath or vow
They'd made since they commenced till
　　now!
They get some fools like you and I
To lift them up to power high,
When this is done those fools they shun,
Their prizes are by others won
While with foul infamy we reek!"
" No. Crawford, no! The one we seek
To place upon this Kingdom's throne,
To break his word was never known!
Sooner he'd lose his life, his head,
And let the dogs his carcass shred,
Than break a promise that he made,
Or falsehood e'er his soul invade!

He knows that we, and we alone,
Can free for him this nation's throne;
Disperse in air that monarch's brow,
Who swayes and rules the nation now.!
He knows that none within the land
As I, so close the king doth stand,
For his most private friend I am,
Know all he seeks to bless or damn;
Know every secret that he knows.
Such faith in me he doth repose
E'en this stately castle, here,
He places solely 'neath my care!
Even though he does all this, I fain
Would see the other monarch reign!
For wider sway and richer spoil
Will then reward my patient toil!
The future monarch also knows
In you the secrets all repose
Of working right that dread machine,
None other knows its whole routine;
That machine whose power shall fling
In air, the palace of a king,
And clear the road for one amain
Who has a juster right to, reign!"

XXX.

As thus he spake, a wily smile
Shot o'er Crawford's face the while,
And when had Ryan ceased, he said,
"Your words would wake to life the dead!
You send a joy through all my soul,
That surges up beyond control,
I feel it through all my being sway!
You have whet my sabre for the fray

And harness'd my steed for battle,
Soon in air yon place shall rattle
With such a deafening din and roar
As never mortal heard before,
And ne'er will hear till time is o'er!
But light a lamp and let us go
And view it in the vaults below.
Come, come along, here are the keys,
You bring the light, I carry these."

XXXI.

A light was lit, and down they sped
Where narrow, winding stairways led
To cellars deep and dark and drear
As ever under castles were;
To a massive iron door they drew,
Its bolts and bars aside they threw,
The door they ope'd, then lightly strode
Along a subterranean road,
A passage dark and drear, which led
To vaults as dark and damp and dread.
Where scarce could breathe a living thing,
Beneath the palace of the king.
These soon they reached, another door
With bolts and bars well covered o'er,
Soon all unlocked, unbarr'd were these
By ponderous, rusty iron keys
Wrought in as strange device as yet
Were ever in a keyhole set;
Soon dupped they wide that iron door
And pass'd those twain the threshold o'er.
Then in a vault as dark and drear
As e'er was fill'd with stagnant air,
Upon the ground around them lay
Eight machines, which did they survey,

Of strange device they all were wrought,
As e'er were shaped by human thought;
One huge wire of shining brass
Round them, and to each machine did
    pass,
From machine to machine did reach,
And for some cause connected each.

XXXII.

" What day, what hour shall it burst,
And send in air this place accurst?
Just fix the time, and sure as fate
We'll make a ruin desolate! "
This Crawford spake, to which replied
Old Ryan, " Crawford, I decide
It be done this night one week from now,
Say just at ten o'clock, I trow
The king makes revelry that night,
And we will put his soul to flight
While mirth and joy is at its height!
Besides, that night I'll be away
On business for the king." " Delay
The hour that brings us fame
Or hasten it, 'tis all the same
To me. Now, I will set the clock
To running. When it strikes, a shock
As of an earthquake shall be heard,
In air these buildings shall be stirr'd
As high as ever mortal dust
From earth was towards the heavens
    thrust! "
He said, and touched a wheel which ran
Like lightning round, and straight began
A motion as of life through all
That dread infernal thing; a tall,

Slim pendulum ticked forth its chime,
And, clock-like, knelled the passing time.
" Think you 'tis sure, and will not fail
These buildings through the air to sail? "
" It's an invention all my own,
And not to any man is known
Its workings, save to me alone.
'Tis sure as death!   Some years ago
I did one in a vessel stow,
That was across the ocean bound;
She sailed, but ne'er a sight nor sound
Of her was ever heard or seen;
None knew her fate but me, I ween!
I know full well that long ere she
Did halfway o'er the ocean flee,
That little trunk I placed on board,
Like peals of hoarded thunder roared!
And all that ship to atoms blew,
As those these walls and roofs will do!
But come; let's move away."

XXXIII.

The door
Secure they closed and locked once more
Swift through that dismal passage past
That was with mildew overcast,
And stank like vaults where rot the dead,
But ere to the outer door they tread,
Like lightning Crawford shot before
And on old Ryan closed the door,
Turn'd on the locks, drew bolt and bar,
So they might sure his exit mar.
Left in the vault that villain hoar,
From whence he never issued more.

Up winding stairs soon Crawford strode,
Where in that room the embers glowed,
Swift on his hat and cloak he threw,
And outward toward the stable drew;
He brought his steed from out the stall
And on him threw his stature tall,
The gate the porter open'd wide.
And swift through it did Crawford ride;
On, on, he spurr'd his steed, until
He gained the summit of a hill,
And rode along a lofty line
Of rocks that o'er a tarn incline,
Where floods with quick-sand slept below.
All covered o'er with sleet and snow;
Here on this high and rocky ground,
He paused and turned his steed around,
And as he tarried here awhile,
He watched the palace with a smile.

XXXIV.

As there he paused, he muttered low,
" If I had time I back would go,
And cleave that hoary porter's head,
And give him to the voiceless dead,
For unless he should die to-night
When yonder buildings take their flight,
When they come well the cause to sift
What in the air yon walls did lift,
He'll tell that I was there to-night,
And put me in an awkward plight.
I should have cleaved his hoary head
Ere from that cursed gate I sped.
I trust he too, to-night will die,
For shortly rocks will wildly fly !

Will make the air most loudly ring
With death dirge of a dying king!
Yes, soon to realms of azure air
Yon stately palace shall repair,
And all who in it sleep to-night
Will never see the morning's light!
Beside his consort rests the king,
Who nestling to his breast doth cling,
As warm around her blooming charms
While half asleep, he winds his arms.
Within a cot their infants sleep,
But ne'er again those babes shall weep;
Their nurse sleeps on the floor above
And dreams of coming bliss and love,
When to her plighted swain she'll bear
Just such sweet offspring bright and fair;
The swain is dreaming of his maid,
By whom he'll never be betrayed;
He sits with her 'neath waving shade,
Their lips warm kisses fast invade;
The porter sleeps the gate beside,
Dreams lords and ladies through it ride,
As oft they have in days of old,
And cast to him some coins of gold;
His steed is dreaming in the stall
Of climbing over mountains tall,
Of leaping through the fearful pass
Of chasms, quicksand, and morass,
Of roaming over deserts broad
Or passing o'er the roaring ford.
All in and round that palace sleeps,
Save old Ryan, perhaps he weeps,
And loudly fills that stagnant air
With yells and damnings of despair!

I trust he has his curses laid
On me, by whom he was betrayed!
Perhaps ere this he's died with fright,
Fear must have overcome him quite;
For all who breathe this vital breath
Dread the approach of grisly death!
All, all, within that palace sleeps,
The watchdog only vigil keeps;
At times his bark comes deep and long,
As if he knew all would soon go wrong!"

XXXV.

Scarce the last words had Crawford spoke,
Than sounds from out that palace broke.
As if there an earthquake had awoke.
Or volcano burst with flame and smoke!
The hills around were shook and riven,
As to the sky those walls were driven;
A moment's space the heavens wore
A crimson glow the hue of gore.
So tall and vast the hissing flame
From out that fatal palace came,
And looked so horrible and fell
It seem'd a bursting up of hell,
Or as if all the flames that dwell
Within the centre of the world,
Were there from out that palace hurl'd,
And all the hoarded din and roar
E'er engendered in its seething core
Had from the boiling centre past
To upper air, in one dread blast;
Tall walls and roofs and lofty spire,
Went up in air with tumult dire!
Through that grim place where Ryan lay,
The blast rushed on with fearful sway,

It and castle from their bases raised,
And high in air dread ruins blazed ;
Then back to earth a flaming hell,
Midst tumult dread the ruins fell,
Down shattered wall, roof and spire,
Dropp'd on earth midst tumult dire !

XXXVI.

Springs from the shock the startled horse,
And forward leaps with headlong force ;
And ere could Crawford draw the rein,
Down, down his charger vaults amain !
Right o'er that tall and sleety line
Of rocks that o'er the tarn incline !
As arrow shot from well-strung bow,
He sped to the abyss below,
Crushed through the robe of frozen snow
To where the yawning quicksands flow,
And right above both horse and man
The closing sand and water ran !
Soon left no utter trace behind
Of steed or form of human kind.
Those rocks rose up so vast and tall,
And so stupendous made the fall.
They must have both been void of breath
And resting in the arms of death,
Ere from that high ridge of rock and snow
They pass'd to the abyss below.
But how that be I cannot tell,
But well I know this fate befell
That gallant steed so fleet and strong,
That like a whirlwind sped along.
Thus past from sight the lofty form
And haughty brow of Crawford Storm.

PART VII.

—

I.

A dark and dismal morning dawn'd,
It seem'd with sleep all nature yawn'd,
With weary drowsiness was rife,
And could not wake to active life:
Upon the tall tree clad with snow,
All moody sat the sable crow;
Abroad through air no chirping bird
On flapping wing that morning stirr'd:
The roe dream'd on the distant hill
Of grassy mound and flowing rill;
The fox lay dreaming in his den
Of well-filled roosts and fattened hen:
The watch-dog in his kennel lay
All still amidst his lair of hay;
No cock around the barn-house crew,
Nor from his roost that morning flew;
The sheep within the distant shed
Lay all as silent as the dead,
From lamb or ewe no bleating came
Nor sound their presence to proclaim;
The silent ox lay on his lair
Dreaming of pastures green and fair,
The goat dreamed with him in the stall,
Of breathless leap o'er stream and wall;
And in his stall the dreaming steed
Cross'd deserts wild with lightning speed,
And in their pen the dreaming swine
Lay all as silent as the kine.

It seem'd that morning's piercing cold
With sleep or silence all controll'd,
O'er skies the clouds lay dark and still,
And poured their hail o'er field and hill.

II.

Perhaps 'twas caused by the fatigue
Of having travelled many a league
O'er hill and dale and wild and moor,
Through storm and blast, the day before,
That made Logan sleep so late that morn;
Perhaps the old man's limbs were worn
And weary with the dreary ride,
And would not be of rest denied;
He did not rise as wont that morn,
Soon as within the east was born
The first faint streaks of coming day,
While yet the morn was dim and gray.
Perhaps his heart felt ease and rest—
With glad content was soothed and blest,
And such should be forevermore,
At having on the eve before
With his own hand, his daughter saved;
Her for whose welfare he had braved
And battled with the ills of life,
To scatter round her comforts rife;
Her whom he loved as pure and wild
As ever parent loved a child—
Bless'd with a blessing deep and strong
As could to a father's soul belong!
What! she, his child, his joy, his love—
Pure as a saint from realms above,
Pure as the light when first 'tis born
Within the golden sky at morn,

Pure as the ether's highest air,
To which no foulness can repair—
Pure as a lily, sweet as love
When first 'twas born in realms above—
Be ta'en from him by a fiend so fell,
And doom'd to a fate as foul as hell!
Be doom'd to a fate more grim and dread
Than babes the hungry tigers shred!
Such thoughts as these through Logan roll,
And busy keep his thinking soul.
When he awoke upon that morn,
Saw night was gone and day was born—
As all alone that old man lay
And watched the morning's dawning ray,
That evening past seem'd unto him
A nightmare horrible and grim—
A dream as drear and wild and strange
As e'er the realm of sleep could range.
And brooding o'er it long he lay,
Nor recked how time had pass'd away
Since first he'd seen the rays of morn
Within the dim horizon born.

III.

'Twas late, that morn, nigh noon, I ween,
Ere Logan from his room was seen—
Ere he had ta'en his morning meal,
Spread by the hand of her whose weal
Was ever foremost in his soul—by day,
By night—where'er he bent his way;
Whose cheering smile aye solaced him
When grew the future drear and dim—
Made the mirkest hours bright,
And lined his darkest clouds with light,

And made the stormy sea of life
Calm down to peace and quiet rife;
Who wept when he went forth, and smiled
With joy when he returned, his child
Who gave back love as pure and true
To him as ever spirit knew.
Many a comely dame and maid
Since in the grave his bride was laid,
Had oft, but all in vain, essayed
With love his spirit to invade.
Like hero sheathed from head to heel
In panoply of purest steel,
And in all feats of battle tried,
He deftly turned their shafts aside;
In his heart, Cupid's arrows found
No vulnerable place to wound.
None in his home should e'er find room
To annoy his child, or cause her gloom;
And e'en had he no daughter there
His dull routine of life to share,
They ne'er had brought John Logan's soul
By any wiles 'neath their control,
Nor found a place his heart beside
Like his lost love, his angel bride;
Whom he believed he'd meet again
Beyond this realm of woe and pain
In endless life on some bright shore
Where they should ne'er be parted more.
But dwell in happiness sublime!
He deem'd he would lie down some time
When least he dream'd that time was near,
Sweet sleep would o'er his senses wear—
Lead him through realms of happy dreams.
Lands rich with bloom and crystal streams,

Where pain and time no subjects keep,
And when he'd wake from that sweet sleep
He'd meet, no more to leave his side,
His mourn'd-for angel—his earthly bride.

IV.

All too wild the blast, the storm too cold,
For a man like him, so worn and old,
To journey forth upon that day
And vengeance on the outlaws lay,
To hound them over hill and glen,
And bring them from their rocky den,
To up tear them, root, branch and stem—
All such treacherous fiends as them,
To hang, or drive them from the shore,
And let them curse the land no more.
But Ragan! where was he?—Around
They searched, but nowhere was he found.
His steed had vanished from the stall,
Gone were his pistols, weapons all;
When he had sped, none there had known,
And the Musgraves, too, were flown.
Out through the window Logan peer'd,
Where bow'd the trees as storms career'd,
Than these naught else his eye could view,
Though far away his gaze he threw.
The time wore on, the morn was past
And evening was approaching fast;
Far down the road his gaze he threw,
But nothing met his eager view
Where'er his longing eye he cast,
But trees that swayed before the blast.

V.

Hark! hark! far, far, across the snow
Bells are ringing, though faint and low,
But louder does their ringing grow
Though angrily the tempests blow
And tear down all that they can throw.
The sounds of bells no deadening know,
And over all their ringings flow.
They are ringing, they are ringing,
Still their music nearer bringing,
And plainer, plainer, sound they still,
Their music bringing up the hill.
And far beyond the waving trees
The eye of Logan plainly sees
Far down the steep and winding road
That leadeth up to his abode,
Of sleighs a lengthy, noisy line,
Fast gliding up the steep incline;
And at their front by him is seen
Some thirty horsemen, full, I ween.
Still faster speeds that cavalcade
Up the sleety, slippery grade.
Foremost of all is Ragan seen,
On his fleet steed of comely mien;
Right soon they Logan's mansion gain,
And round the old man crowd amain.

VI.

Right soon doth Logan's willing ear
Their strange, wondrous tidings hear,
For all the Grangers far and near
Had gathered, though the day was drear,

In one firm mass, compact and strong,
And did throughout the mountains throng;
Scoured the country far and wide,
Sought those who had the laws defied;
Described the scene old Bolton's bield
Had to their searching eyes revealed,
Told of the horrid sight they saw,
Which almost struck them dumb with awe;
Where once had stood that loathsome den
Where died Wallace and those other men,
They saw the place to ashes burn'd,
The bodies unto cinders turn'd—
All so completely singed and charr'd
They mortal recognition marr'd;
Which was Wallace, Down, or Hugh Le-
    nore,
'Twas vain for mortal to explore;
No eye would ever know them more,
Howe'er it searched their bodies o'er.
Of all those fiends they had some clue,
Save Crawford, naught of him they knew;
For him they'd searched around, around,
But Crawford nowhere could be found.
And said the Sheriff, who did appear
Among that throng of Grangers there,
" Crawford, I solemnly can swear
Was not in Wallace's abode,
Not once his presence there he showed,
The two whole nights and one whole day,
I did amongst those villains stay !
I drank Judge Down, and all in there,
As drunk as ever mortals were;
Nor sound nor scene they could discern;
I stayed with them in hopes to learn

Who some foul burglaries had done
Within our city.   I spun
Long yarns with them, sung, drank and
    swore,
Did whiskey down like water pour;
With them a chummy I became,
Whate'er they did I did the same;
But not one word from them I caught
To form a clue to what I sought.
I left them in the dead of night,
For I was sick and worn outright.
But when I left, upon the floor
Each did in drunken stupor snore,
The massive stove glowed warm and
    bright
And round the barroom threw its light,
And when I left them on that night
All seem'd in order, trim and right,
As just might any barroom show;
What caused the fire, I do not know,
And was surprised to see this morn
Things round there looking so forlorn.
Judge Down lay close the stove beside,
And near him did some others bide,
It, he or they may have o'erturn'd,
And thus themselves to cinders burned.
But how it be I do not know,
Nor need we care for their o'erthrow,
But glory that their doom is o'er,
And that they'll trouble us no more.
But Crawford was not there, I know,
Himself to us he'll some day show;
Who captures him, alive or dead,
Ere from this day a year has sped,

Shall have whate'er he choose to ask
For having thus performed that task.

VII.

To the hut of Hugh Lenore we drew,
Had of his hag a final view—
For when we open thrust the door
She with grim death was fighting sore;
But ere her lips were sealed in death,
Revealed she with her latest breath,
'Twas Bolton and her spouse, Lenore,
Who years ago, perhaps a score,
Your stately barns and buildings burn'd,
And cattle into cinders turn'd;
'Twas them who stole your boy and sped
Away with him for Etheldred,
Who at that time lived in the town,
Next building to his Judgeship, Down;
Who with the child fled on that night,
To unknown regions took his flight,
Some secret purpose to fulfill;
And says if Etheldred is still
Alive and can be found, and will
Divulge the truth, then you will know
All 'bout your offspring's weal or woe,
Learn whether he's alive or dead,
Where rest his bones, or footsteps tread."

VIII.

While thus he spake, far down the hill
Where trees swayed to the tempest still,
The Sheriff's eagle eye espied
Along the road two horsemen ride.
" Haste, and look yonder!" loud he cried,
" If to me my vision has not lied,

By all the souls on earth, I vow,
Yon foremost man is Crawford now!
He doth exactly like him ride,
And doth as nobly steed bestride!
Although his soul is grim and fell—
Is in itself a horrid hell,
Ne'er better horseman drew a rein
Till now, across a charger's mane!
Knights of old, of which the poets tell,
Methinks ne'er rode a steed so well.
Did ne'er so firm and solid sit—
Erect and square the saddle fit,
While battling in the tourney's ring
To win the daughter of a king;
Or when they rushed for high renown
And won a kingdom and a crown."

IX.

Ere this was said, upon his steed
Had Ragan sprung with lightning speed,
Struck deep his spurs, and with a bound
Shot forth from those who gaped around,
And muttered low as forth he sped,
"I'll lose my life or lay him dead!
Dead or alive, I'll carry him,
A trophy unto vengeance grim!
His life's the prize, that prize be mine,
Or I'll not see this day's decline!"
He said, and death had surely been.
While yet were twenty yards between
Those men, had not Earl Ragan seen
A comely visage and a mien
Far other than he sought, I ween,
And rushed for with a hate so keen!

But too tremendous was the force
With which then onward sped his horse
For him to stop him on that road,
Which was with sleet all overflowed ;
His speed was all too wild and high,
Like bolt of lightning shot he by !
His instant death he there had brought,
If then so wild a deed he wrought ;
For if he'd caused his steed to fall,
They both had slid o'er boulders tall,
Where ne'er did tree nor vintage grow,
Where yawn'd a dread abyss below ;
Nor did he pause till far away
His steed had carried him, where lay
Beyond the hill a level plain,
And starkly there drew in the rein.

X.

Meanwhile that unknown horseman rode
On, climbed the hill to that abode,
And there himself from saddle flung
And lightly o'er the threshold sprung,
Strode on, nor head nor body bowed
To any of that gaping crowd ;
Strode in with high and haughty head,
And firm, elastic stalwart tread ;
And looked around that ample hall
As he were master of it all.
Tall was his form, erect and broad,
And limbs to frame did well accord,
He seem'd of strength, from head to heel,
A perfect model to reveal ;
From side to side, through all his length
He seem'd activity and strength ;

And his clean-shaved, frank, open face,
Bespoke him born of noble race.
Who, who is he? the whisper ran
Among that throng, from man to man.
Who, who is he? but none can tell.
His gaze on them a moment fell,
And in that glance eyed every man;
Then with commanding voice began:

XI.

" Does here a man named Logan dwell?
John Logan; can any of you tell?"
" He does, and I here am that man!"
With voice which all as haughty ran,
John Logan swift to him replied,
And rapidly approached his side.
" If you are he, my business, then,
Is with you, none of these other men;
So please to grant a moment's space
With me, within some private place."
A door John Logan opes anon
And forthwith led the stranger on;
Into a wide and ample hall
Strode then those figures broad and tall;
Closed to the door secure was thrown,
And those two men were all alone.
The father and the son had met at last,
Though twenty weary years had past
Since fate asunder them had cast,
And made a difference all so vast.

XII.

A moment, and but a moment's space,
The young man viewed the old man's face,

And as he did, a beaming smile
His manly visage shed the while,
And with a voice all soft and sweet of tone.
Quite changed to what before he'd shown,
And bowing low to the hoary man,
He his business thus began :
" Read this, before a word I say,
'Twill all my business here convey
To you direct." With that he lay
A letter in the old man's hand,
Sealed tight, and tied with silken band,
Which swift John Logan open tore
And spread it wide his gaze before,
And thus he read.—
  *   *   *   *   *   Since I took your son
Till now, just twice ten years have run.
And while those weary years have flown,
I trust enough of grief you've known !
Enough of anguish, care and woe,
To recompense all hate I know,
And feel, and have for you ! So now
I'll glad your heart and light your brow !
I send you back a soul and form
As perfect e'er as life can warm.
John Logan, no such form and soul,
Had ever reared 'neath your control.
Thus, injuries I have repaid,
Which were by you upon me laid !
Take back your babe; with him I'm done;
My sands of life are almost run,
But still I hate you, as of old,
With hatred lasting, deep, untold !
Take back your child ! My tale is done.
My journey to an ending spun !
Guy Etheldred

XIII.

Was it joy or woe,
Or some strange thoughts of long ago,
That surged the while through Logan's
soul,
And bowed it neath their strong control?
For with surprise profound—amazed,
Upon the youth the old man gazed!
There, moveless as some statue stood
That's carved of stone by sculptor good.
The color fled his manly face,
Left it white as his locks apace.
Amazed, surprised, he fix'd his stare
Upon the young man standing there,
Where stood the vigor, health and bloom,
Tall form and chest of ample room,
He did in ruddy prime assume,
Ere wrecked with age and sorrow's gloom.
And it he viewed as still and dumb,
As though death had life o'ercome,
And ceased through all that form to thrill.
With silence all as stern and still,
The young man fix'd his rigid gaze
Upon his sire, with amaze
Retracing every line of form
And face, though bent with age and storm,
The ruins of himself.   Though gray
With age and woe and worn away,
Still all majestic in decay.

XIV.

An ample space did they survey
Each other o'er and o'er; at last
A tremor through old Logan past,

And thus he said : " A certain sign
Will manifest if you be mine.
When scarce two fleeting years had shed
Their seasons o'er my infant's head,
Where played he on the ground one day
It chanced a wild steer made his way,
And him caught up upon his horn.
Right fearful was his shoulder torn ;
Deep to the bone the sharp horn gored,
And left a wound, grim, long and broad.
And even when the wound was healed
A fearful seam was there revealed,
Which no art of leach-craft could displace,
Nor fleeting time shall e'er efface.
And if your shoulder on the right
Reveals to mortal such a sight,
Then I will take it as a sign
You are the child ; that you are mine ! "

XV.

Swift from his tall and comely form
That young man doffed his garments
        warm,
Laid all his brawny shoulders bare—
The ghastly seam of yore was there !
Smote with the sign, his doubts amain
Disperse like mirky clouds of rain
When Sol in all his splendor reigns
And pours his warmth o'er hills and plains.
His soul within him melts. No more
·His knees and joints his frame upbore ;
His feeble form his arms alone
Support, around his offspring thrown !
But these, too, to sustain him failed ;
He swoons, with whelming joy assailed ;

And sinks upon that lov'd one's breast,
Who to his heart that form caress'd.
Soon as returning life regains
Control, the blood sweeps through his
    veins,
" Yes," he whispers low, " Yes, I believe
God pities all who mourn and grieve!
By mortals He's not understood,
But He is just and He is good!
Yes, yes! you are my long lost son,
O'er whose dread loss my life has run
One ceaseless stream of lasting woe,
Which day nor night would respite know!
Yes, all your mien and bearing shows
It is my blood that in you flows!
Thank God, He did my child restore!
And may we ne'er be parted more
Till my career on earth is run!
When we've immortal life begun,
May we two meet upon some shore,
Be never, never parted more!
Oh! through what sorrows have I run,
In seeking you, my son! my son!
Thank God! those pangs and woes are
    o'er!
That Heaven decreed we'd meet once
    more!"
So o'er his offspring spake that man,
While fast his tears of rapture ran;
While he clasp'd and kiss'd his stately boy,
And wept with overflowing joy;
Their tears of joy commingling flow
And rapture doth commingling glow,
While fall the old man's locks of snow
On those that fewer winters know,

And murmurs flow, "My son!" my son!"
And "Father!" mingling with them run.

XVI.

When their first pangs of joy were past,
Or into milder mood were cast,
"Oh! tell me all!" the old man cried.
As he his tears of rapture dried,
"Within what regions you've been thrown,
What life and trials have you known?
Tell, tell it all to me, and how
It chances you are with me now?
For this all seems to me a dream,
Where no reality doth gleam!
Where only wildest fiction burns!"
He said, and straight the son returns:

XVII.

"'Twere long, and needless, now, I ween,
To tell you all the sights I've seen,
Though all the time we've parted been—
So many seasons intervene,
Enough of time I back will go
To suit the present, just to show
How, who I am I came to know,
Who on my mind that knowledge threw!
The rest some other time will do:
A week ago Guy Etheldred,
Whose note to you but now you read,
Was quailing with the pangs of death;
But ere from him had past his breath
He called me to his dying bed,
And thus in feeble accents said:
"My boy, my life is nearly done,
My fleeting sands have almost run!

So when my breathing shall be o'er
And life in me you see no more,
Take you, my boy, these letters twain,
And forward with them speed amain
To those they are address'd; and mind,
You fail not both of them to find:
One is your sire! Years I've made
You fancy I was him. Betrayed
You into such belief—deceived
And blinded you! Yes, you believed
From me your source of being drew.
Think so no more! It's all untrue!
John Logan is your father's name!
I stole and brought you from the same
When you were but a little child,
For reasons all too strange and wild
For me to breathe in mortal ear,
And none those reasons e'er shall hear!
They shall in secret pass away
With me, where'er my spirit stray.
But boy, of all the years you've seen
In company with me, I ween,
I never did to you a deed
By night or day, that you might heed
As any way at all unkind.
I ne'er did thwart nor cross your mind;
All I've done was for your good;
I aye your steadfast friend have stood,
And this to me you'll witness bear,
E'en when my voice no more you hear.
To you I leave all, all the hoard
That fortune did to me accord;
You know where every mite is stored,
So take it hence with you abroad.

But weep not when I've pass'd away,
No sorrow show, by night or day,
I would not have my spirit see
A mortal ever grieve for me.
I loathe, detest and hate my kind,
Despise them, body, soul and mind!
I want no sympathy, no show—
No slightest signs of human woe
Ever bestowed upon my tomb,
No sorrow round my narrow room!
And one more thing, take solemn heed
Ne'er night nor day in any deed
Long as on earth your life shall span,
Be you a partner with that man
Who sometimes journeys here, we call
Crawford Storm. Thyself wall
Securely 'gainst him every way,
And shun him ever, night and day ;
'Gainst him be ever on your guard,
For he is cursed and evil starr'd !
Many a deed I know of him
Would send him to the gallows grim !
Now, I have told you all, take heed,
And follow in the path I lead.
Farewell ! " With that the old man's
        breath
Grew weak, and soon was hushed in death.
I followed him unto his tomb,
And left him in his narrow room.
Then forward from that land I sped
To do the bidding of the dead,
And journeyed here. And this is how
It chances we are meeting now.

XVIII.

Soon were the tidings noised around
That Logan's long lost son was found;
Swift as the falling of a star
That news was carried wide and far;
O'er hill and dale, o'er forest, field,
Through stately mansion, lonely bield,
From mouth to mouth the tidings flew,
Till all within that country knew
The lost was found! The much deplored
And sought-for stolen one restored!
Who had mouth to speak, ears to hear,
All told and heard it far and near.
Like all such news, where'er it flew,
It quite some other version knew—
On every tongue the story grew,
Not wholly false nor wholly true;
For all mankind, nor age nor youth
Will ever stick to solid truth.;
Each has his own peculiar style,
As well as gesture, frown or smile,
His tale to tell, be it a lie,
Or something true, as man must die;
In private and in public place,
With wild amazement in each face,
The tidings gathered as they roll'd,
No sooner heard than sooner told.
An ember cast upon the waste
Midst leaves, to ruddy blaze will haste,
The flame the woody valley fills
And onward mounts the neighboring hills.
O'er peaks the spreading torrent goes
Till all the hills it overflows;

This way and that it flies and turns,
And over all in fury burns—
With a roar o'er wold and field,
And where aught will to its fury yield.
So spread the news that country round,
That Logan's long lost child was found :
" Roderic's found! old Logan's child ! "
Spread o'er that country fast and wild.

XIX.

Onward sped untiring time,
And dreary winter left that clime;
No more across its sleet and snow
On breath of icy winds, the flow
Of music from the loud sleigh-bells
Upon the ear at midnight swells ;
Departed for a little time,
Is this loved pastime of that clime.
Sweet spring has come with all her robe
Of glory to enhance the globe;
Rose and violet bloom o'er the field,
And to the air their sweetness yield ;
On lonely wold and hill and dell,
Sweet violets the peasants smell ;
Beside the stream the lily blooms,
And waving o'er the harebell looms,
The forests all alive are seen,
And waving with their glowing green,
And all around the air is stirr'd
With sweetest music of the bird.
Sweet is the scene o'er dale and hill,
By mossy rock and flowing rill ;
Sweet is the view o'er pastures green,
Where skipping lambs and sheep are seen ;

Sweet is the view both far and near,
Each sight we see, each sound we hear
Shows spring in all her charms arrayed
As sweet as ever yet surveyed;
As grand, as beautiful, sublime,
As ever yet was known to time;
Where cultivated fields are seen,
For these mongst pastures intervene,
Glows with dark green the waving grain,
Encumbering the fertile plain.
The owner's careful hand and toil
Is plainly stamped on all the soil,
On plant and tree his care is shown,
On all within that region grown;
No empty spot escapes the care
Of the wise, thrifty owner there.

XX.

'Twas spring, I said, and flowers shed
Their sweets on air where'r it fled;
That it seem'd all things glowed with mirth
That sprouted from the teeming earth,
And made her bosom throb with joy,
As had John Logan's for his boy;
Said every mute and living thing
Was gladdened with the glowing spring,
And on its rich and fertile lair
The grain waved to the wholesome air.
Gave promise when the harvest came
An ample yielding of the same,
To prove within some future hour
Its mighty recreative power.
And so was man glad with the spring,
As birds that made their music ring

Through forests waving green and tall,
And round the eves of mansion wall.
Yes, man and woman, young and old,
Delighted did the spring behold ;
Gray matrons with their ample brood
Were all of gay and happy mood ;
And old men sang and laughed with joy,
And wished themselves once more a boy ;
Boys wished that they were only men,
And thought how free they could be then
To round the May-Pole skip and spring,
To dance, to frolic, and to sing.
The maiden eyed her chosen youth,
Thought him all manliness and truth ;
And he glanced on his blushing maid,
Saw her with every charm arrayed,
While round the May-Pole deck'd with
    flowers
They danced away the fleeting hours.
And many a spinster well in years
Around the May-Pole too, appears ;
Though men have neglected her so long,
Yet, yet her hope is bright and strong ;
Though none as yet her hand has sought,
Nor loving homage to her brought,
Yet, round as gay she skips and springs
As do the younger, fairer things ;
On young and old she sweetly smiles,
But alas, alas, she none beguiles !
Now, Hope, thou heaven-born power !
Ne'er let despair within her lower,
Nor 'neath that grisly tyrant cower,
But fill her soul through every hour.
The one she seeks for may she meet,
And he make her happiness complete.

XXI.

Bright was the day, the balmy breeze
Was stirring midst the leafy trees,
The clover blossoms fill'd the air
With sweetness all beyond compare,
And the countless flowers that bloom'd,
With richness rare the breeze perfumed.
The sun shone warm o'er dale and hill,
Laughed bright on stream and glowing
    rill,
While floods of song and music's thrill
Did echoing plain and forest fill ;
And round a May-Pole richly clad
With all the flowers Nature had,
With all she ever brought to glad
Poor earth, with deserts lone and sad,
A mighty throng of gay and young,
Both maids and youths, danced, skipped
    and sung ;
So merrily the time employed,
It seem'd all woe had been destroyed—
Sent from the world, with all its pain,
And ne'er would visit earth again.
And to the scene so bright and gay,
Came with his daughter, Sheriff Fay.
" Daughter," he said, while yet away
From that grand festival array,
" If love for Ragan yet you feel,
Take my advice, that flame conceal ;
And let none know 'twas ever felt,
Just let it from your bosom melt,
As doth the flake of fleecy snow
When warm on it the spring suns glow.

Your love and his will never meet
Within commingling union sweet;
It won't, like wine and water blend,
Nor mingle as all love should wend.
As you broke the trust I in you laid,
Through it his flight from dungeon
        made,
So, by him will you be yet betrayed.
You'll hear when you expect it least
That all his love for you has ceased!
Yea, every mite and atom fled,
And that he's Logan's daughter wed.
And even should you be his wife,
You'd lead a most infernal life!
For all the love would be one side,
And that within his gentle bride.
He's after Logan's child, I know,
So on that journey let him go,
Nor to it slightest hinderance throw.
But see you after Roderick, now;
He's better looking, that I'll vow!
And has far more of ready cash—
And that cannot be reckon'd trash
By any maid who'd pave her way
Unto an easy life and gay.
Riches crown married lives with love,
Lifts them up earth's dull cares above;
But poverty sinks them below,
Where hustle toil and care and woe.
It is the most annoying life,
To be a poor man's slaving wife,
That any mortal woman led
Since first the race to man were wed.
It's all quite nice for bards to tell

Of vine-wreathed cot in shady dell,
Where loving wedded couples dwell!
How both the husband and his wife
Toil on through all their earthly life,
In perfect happiness and love,
Keeping their minds all cares above;
I tell you, child it's all a lie!
And hope you'll ne'er such nonsense try.
You'll find when want treads on the floor,
All love will straight fly out the door'
And fly so very far away
She back will scarcely ever stray.
If you would act discreet and wise,
Look to Roderick, as I advise;
He's of that throng the only prize!
I've watched him oft when you were near,
And in manner he did so appear,
That were I on my oath I'd swear
Your charms had all besieged his soul—
Thrall'd him with love complete and whole.
I'm old in years, and I have seen
Of love and wooing, lots, I ween,
And am not easily deceived;
That he loves you I've long believed.
Now, daughter, you are young and fair
As any of those maidens there,
With voice more sweet than any bird
Whose notes the breeze of morning heard,
Or yet the air of nature stirr'd!
Whate'er you speak, in every word
A soft and subtile music lives,
Such, methinks, as God to seraph gives!
And from your lips a glory breathes,
Such as might come from rainbow wreathes.

So go, my child, midst yonder throng
With hope and courage bright and strong,
In glowing pride of maidenhood,
As yet on earth has ever stood,
And win and bring with you away,
Completely bowed beneath your sway,
The only prize that can be found,
Howe'er you search them round and round,
Midst all that throng of smiling youth;
And this I swear to be the truth!
Now, go, my child, upon your way;
Your sweetest smiles to him display,
And keep you out of Ragan's path;
Though should you meet, no sign of wrath
For him, nor least displeasure show;
But let your smiles for Roderick glow.
Now go, I've nothing else to say."

XXII.

Light as air she sped upon her way.
How well that bright and lovely maid
The bidding of that voice obeyed
Was shortly unto him revealed.
Nor was it from that throng concealed;
Where'er the maiden moved that day,
Beside her Roderick made his way;
And long before the evening mist
Had either hill or valley kiss'd,
Or ere those sounds of frolic died,
That maid was Roderick's promised bride.

XXIII.

The spring was gone, and summer flown,
The autumn all his leaves had strown,

And gathered on his lap sublime
The glories of a year of time.
And winter, icy, drear and lone,
Was mounting fast his hoary throne,
And over realms of sleet and snow
Did music from the sleigh-bells flow ;
By night and day their sound was heard,
Through icy air their music stirr'd,
As in the spring the song of bird ;
Far over snowy heath and holt
Noisy sleighs and fleet chargers volt,
And song and laughter floats around,
With mirth in every sight and sound.

XXIV.

'Twas night, and calm the frosty air
Lay sleeping on its icy lair ;
Through lofty forests clad with snow
No noisy breath of breezes blow,
Through them no sounds of wind is heard,
By it no single branch is stirr'd,
For all the breeze has hushed its breath,
And sleeps as still and cold as death.
No sign of cloud is seen on high
Through all the regions of the sky ;
The full, round moon in all her glow
Serenely casts her light below
On streams and mountains' icy heads,
Sparkling, silvery light she sheds ;
With quivering sheen the glowing rills
Like flowing silver, line the hills,
And icy leaves resplendent gleam
Beneath the all-enlivening beam,

And 'neath her rays like silver glow
The never-ending piles of snow.
Unnumbered stars in glory shine
And cast o'er earth their light divine,
Steady they blaze, or twinkling glow,
From pole to pole their glories show
Fair was the night as ever yet
Has beam'd on earth or mortal met,
Since first from out Creation's plan
Sprung forth that animal called man.

XXV.

I said all nature lay at rest,
As sleeping babe on mother's breast,
And so it did, all save that part
Controlled by human hand and heart,
And this was just as full of din
As waters of a roaring linn.
By maid and youth, the snow-clad earth
Resounded with the sounds of mirth,
The young, the old, the brave, the fair,
With mirth and laughter shook the air;
Danced many a rosy maiden's eye
With joy, like twinkling stars on high.

XXVI.

Behold the stately edifice
At base of yon tall precipice,
With lofty steeple reared on high
As if it sought to reach the sky!
Its glowing point beneath the light
The moonbeams cast on it so bright,
Glitters on its tall throne afar
As brilliant as the sheenest star.

Of dark gray stone is rear'd the wall
Of yonder building broad and tall;   ·
Of slate is built its lofty roof,
And is to flame and tempest proof;
Taking that building joint by joint,
From base to topmost steeple point,
It is as grand Cathedral pile
On which as yet did moonbeams smile.
Within the place is light as day,
As lit by Sol's all-piercing ray
When not a cloud obscures his beam
And warm he smiles on hill and stream.
And in that wide and spacious door
A constant stream of people pour,
As waters that are onward drawn
To where doth spacious chasm yawn,
Still onward sweep in steady flow
Till all the space is fill'd below;
So in that church the people pour,
Until the place will hold no more.
Both young and old, the brave and fair
That country round, are gathered there.
Their eyes are bright, their faces smile,
For rapture reigns in them the while,
Nor is there a care-worn brow nor face
Seen mongst them all within that place;
Seated, or standing 'long the aisles,
With joy each face serenely smiles.
With stirring notes the organs chime
With sacred tones of hymns sublime,
Airs sweet as music in her prime
Will e'er conceive till ceases time;
Nor is mongst all the organs sound,
The hymns from human voices drown'd;

These, like a holy anthem pour
Above a distant torrent's roar.

XXVII.

The organs ceased their holy sound
And all the hymns were hushed around,
And all within that sacred place
No sound is heard a little space,
Save breathing of the human breath,
All, all, a space, is still as death.
With parted lips and straining eyes,
All look to where a group arise—
A little group of scarce a score,
Who halt the altar rail before.
Among them Sheriff Fay is seen,
And hoary Logan's comely mien,
But who are those that on them lean,
Each blushing sweet as Beauty's Queen?
Whose faces tell that feelings dull
Within their souls are void and null,
Whose flowing robes of snowy mull
Fall around necks and arms as fair
As yet were fann'd by vital air,
Whose floating, snowy veils stream o'er
Faces sweet as ever veiled before,
Whose brows are deck'd with bridal
    wreathes,
Choice as those 'neath which Flora
    breathes;
Each blushes like the Queen of Flowers,
When smiling midst her choicest bowers,
And mirth and joy her features don.
Who are they? Answer comes anon :
Mary Logan, and Ellen Fay!
Their lovers close beside are they :

By Mary's arm is Ragan seen,
By Ellen's, Roderick's comely mein.
Each kneel'd a space, and o'er each head
The sacred rite and prayer was said;
To maidens' hands they quickly bring
The round, the never-ending ring.

XXVIII.

The prayer was said, the rite was done,
Each happy couple stood as one.
Then did the merry organs chime
Their tones of prayer and praise sublime,
In glory of that happy time.
From nave to aisle, from aisle to nave,
Did whelming floods of music wave—
From steeple to foundation stone
The place was shook with music's tone,
As by a tempest strong and grim;
Voice after voice joined in the hymn,
Until the sound of music rose
Far louder than the noise that goes
Before the tempest o'er the deep,
And wakes the ocean from its sleep.
Voice after voice joined in the song,
Till it rose an anthem deep and strong—
Till all that sacred place within
Seem'd bursting with its holy din!
Still swell'd it on and shook the air,
Till left each bright and happy pair.

XXIX.

Forward the stream of time has drawn,
To gulfs that never cease to yawn—
To pits that drink the flood of years,
As caves down which the torrent tears,

Which never, never, never fill,
But are forever empty still!
And which shall never fill till time
Shall startle at the tones sublime—
That knell on earth, her funeral lay,
And she with earth shall pass away.
And through the fleeting flight of time
Has Logan lived to hear the chime
Of merry voices round his knee,
And there his children's children see.
Long years of peace on earth he found,
A life with every blessing crown'd,
His mind at ease, his body sound,
With wealth and plenty scattered round;
The rich reward and glowing spoil
Of all his years of thrift and toil.
Sublime in faith with God he stood,
And strove to do his fellows good;
If they had faults, he'd mildly chide,
And ever seek their faults to hide,
Though far from virtue's path they slid;
And when he prayed—which oft he did—
Full one-half his prayer was given
For others' weal. If men are riven
Of their sins on earth by the prayers
Of other men as well as theirs,
Then many a human creature's soul
When death brought it to its final goal,
Placed it before the Judgment Bar,
Where sins be known, whate'er they are,
They learned before that Awful Throne
His prayers had saved them, his alone.
Gray with years and hoary weight of age,
He past from off this earthly stage,

Wept, mourned for, honored and revered,
To every human heart endeared.

XXX.

Long lived the jolly Sheriff Fay,
And kept all grief and care at bay;
He sang his song and quaft his wine,
And ever on the best would dine;
Riches he had, so choicest food
Alone, did soothe his hungry mood.
He loved his grog, perhaps, too well,
And none within that land did dwell
Could fill his glass unto the brim
And drain it down as oft as him!
Many a man he drunk has made,
And him beneath the table laid,
And while he there in stupor snored,
Would Fay sit up beside the board;
And with some other mortal drunk,
Who also 'neath the table sank.
And when the sky with morn grew gray,
Though drunk around his comrades lay,
He could arise and march along,
His breakfast eat and sing a song;
Could dance a jig or run a mile,
Or with his grand-sons play awhile.
Next to his food and whiskey bowl,
Loved games at cards with all his soul—
And there he never lost his vole.
He lived to be a hoary man,
And all his days in pleasure ran
Long as on earth his being stood,
And if no harm, yet little good
He did unto his fellow man,
Through all that life so broad of span.

XXXI.

Long, happy lived the wedded pairs,
Time gathered round them many heirs,
Both rosy girls and ruddy boys,
Which crowned their lives with countless
    joys.
And may they all as fruitful be
As is the fair and healthy tree,
Whose roots are deep in fertile ground
With crystal waters flowing round,
Which never fails to bloom in spring
And ample fruit in season bring.

XXXII.

All trace of Down was soon forgot—
And even o'er the very spot
His stately mansion once was seen—
That building of such com.ly mien—
A highway of that town was made,
And it in dark oblivion laid;
His memory sank in deepest shade;
At last it did from mortals fade;
He left no slightest trace behind
To tell his fame to human kind.
And shortly, Wallace, too, was cast,
Midst things of the forgotten past;
From men his memory decayed,
Did from their minds completely fade,
As watered valleys reck no more
Of droughts of years forever o'er.
And on that very spot of ground
Where once his inn and barns were found
With their tall, massive walls of stone,
Now is the paupers' graveyard known;

The stone that formed each building's wall
Make round the spot enclosure tall.

XXXIII.

Long was that country searched around,
In hopes that Crawford might be found;
Full thirty years had past, and more,
Ere all that search was given o'er.
They all believed that he had fled—
Unto some unknown region sped;
And that the day would yet appear
That they would see him mongst them
    there—
That he would surely mongst them come,
His hate and vengeance deal on some.
And armed were men for combat grim,
Lest they should ever meet with him.
Whene'er a barn at night was burn'd
Their thoughts were straight on Crawford
    turn'd,
No matter what the deed of crime
That there was done at any time,
If he who did it was not known
The crime was straight on Crawford
    thrown.
Yes, either him or some ally
When it was done was surely nigh,
Was there the universal cry
Mongst rich and poor, the low and high.
If at night a charger shied,
They deem'd that steed had Crawford
    eyed;
That he was mongst the bushes there,
And straight to meet him they'd prepare.

And when at night a noise was heard,
"Twas thought that somewhere Crawford
    stirr'd ;
They swore they heard his voice of doom
Whispering through the midnight gloom.
Thus till many years had sped
He was their terror and their dread.
Whene'er was seen the track of horse
On lonely, unfrequented course,
In byways, over glen or hill,
By grassy mound or flowing rill,
Through field or marsh, or forest vast,
'Twas thought that there had Crawford
    past ;
And straight for him keen search was
    made,
No matter where those horse-tracks
    strayed.
So long they searched that realm for him,
Wherever man could climb or swim.
Thenceafter never robber band
Found resting place within that land.
No hill so wild, no glen so lone,
It was not to those Grangers known ;
If hole or cave there met their view
They stayed not till they searched it
    through.
A common danger linked and bound
In close ally those Grangers round.
No stranger there they could discern,
But him at once they questioned stern—
From whence he came and whither bound,
What manner he his living found
And if his answers were not clear,
Soon forced to quit that country there,

And never tread that land again,
Or he should don a ball and chain.
The Devil's Rift those Grangers sought,
And quite a change in it was wrought.
Its granite walls were pierced and drill'd,
Its chasms deep with rocks were fill'd ;
A safe and solid road was drawn
O'er pits that once did frightful yawn,
Made it another aspect don ;
And as fleetfooted time sped on,
And round her wheel of changes spun,
A railroad through that pass was run,
And there it stands unto this day,
In that once feared and hated way.
Through it the roaring engines fly,
With them I'll prove I do not lie.

XXXIV.

Long o'er those forests dark and drear
From morn till night those old one's peer,
For still bright hope their souls beguiled,
That they would someday see their child.
And soon as morn the skies would span
Their watch for him they straight began ;
And not till after set of sun,
And all those woods grew dark and dim.
Black night had wrapp'd the world in peace.
Did their sad, fruitless vigils cease.
Through weary days and months and years,
Amidst alternate smiles and tears,
They watched those forests lone and drear,
For him who never did appear.
Still whiter grew each hoary head,
Still slower, feebler, grew their tread,

Till either form was bent and worn,
And seem'd almost of being shorn.
They lived to see a vast old age
Ere ta'en from off this mortal stage;
But on one bright and early morn
While snows did all those woods adorn,
And sleet lay thick on all the ground,
Dead on their couch those two were found.
Still hand in hand and side by side,
As they had lived so they had died;
Together, left this dismal sphere,
As was their wont to journey here.
Yes, side by side, and hand in hand,
Together trod that unknown land,
Upon whose solemn, silent shore,
'Tis said, we meet and part no more;
And feel no pangs of doubt and pain,
Where fleeting time shall cease to reign.
And may they there their Crawford find,
A soul in purity enshrined,
A spirit cleaned of every crime
It did while midst the realms of time;
A spirit beautiful and bright,
Of all its sins made clean and white,
By some strange, wondrous, process known
To God, and unto God alone,
Which sin shall into goodness turn
As wood doth into ashes burn,
Or solid ice to liquid run
Beneath the glowing of the sun;
Or hardest rocks in nature found
Are into finest powder ground
Through time and storm, then scattered
    wide,
And never more on earth espied;

Or the unsightly, rusty ore,
Doth from the blazing furnace pour
A liquid mass of glowing steel,
Which doth to metal strong congeal,
And forms at last the gleaming sword
That rules and awes a nation broad.
God made all evil and all good,
By him alone they're understood.
Through Him sin in purity shall end
And all in holiness shall blend,
But how, finite minds can't comprehend.
And if their prayers on earth availed,
With which they daily God assailed,
They'll surely meet in realms above,
Where all is holiness and love,
That son of theirs for whom they grieved,
Till God their wretchedness relieved.
My task is done, my tale is told;
Now critics, howl! fret, rave, and scold!
Like hungry wolves on frozen wold,
O'er which the clouds of night are roll'd,
Who scent afar the noisy fold;
But fear too well the shepherd bold,
Who there doth nightly vigil hold,
For them to venture through the cold.
Yet critics, great, both young and old,
Who ne'er a sentence kind could mol l
Save unto ye was shown some gold,
Farewell; I care not how is doled
To me the praise by ye controll'd,
For it is cheaply bought or sold;
And when o'er this your eyes have stroll'd
You'll see this craft is strongly poled.

www.ingramcontent.com/pod-product-compliance
Lightning Source LLC
Chambersburg PA
CBHW021043030726
47496CB00006B/1658